THINGS COME *Together*

Darrius Williams

Things Come Together

Published by TJS Publishing House
www.tjspublishinghouse.com
contact@tjspublishinghouse.com

Published in the United States of America

ISBN-13: 978-1-952833-31-1
ISBN-10: 1-952833-31-0

Table of Contents

CHAPTER 1

Dallas, TEXAS

FRIDAY EVENING.

The sound of blaring horns and the verbal insults of drivers toward one another swamped the city during the 5pm hour. The impatience of people in rush hour traffic would lead someone to believe that it was a new phenomenon. People were anxious to get home, anxious to relax, and release all of the stress brought onto them during the work week. Often when people were preparing to hop on the expressway, they would always at least for a moment have to see an elegant giant of glass in the heart of downtown. The building, which belonged to a company known as Anomaly Automation, was visible from almost anywhere and difficult to miss. It adopted the finesses of modern design while retaining the architectural class of the previous age. Anomaly was a company that many strived to become a part of; a company that continued to dominate the marketplace. It was the golden stamp of approval when listed on an applicant's resume. Those privileged to become a part of the company often worked late hours and went above and beyond to build their reputation and cement their careers. The entire culture of the company was saturated in competition and cutting loose ends, there was no looking forward to unwinding and relaxation.

Friday evenings were everything but relaxed, and this Friday was no different. The executives and certain department heads for Anomaly were called to stay late due to an emergency meeting scheduled by the CEO. The executive boardroom was a room that a select few were given the opportunity to experience, and once someone was able to experience it, they understood why. A lot of money was put into the design of the boardroom. One of the walls was covered with a huge flat screen that spanned across it, like that of a jumbo screen in a major sports arena. A long dark marble table, covered in journals, notepads, smart phones, and laptops, stretched from one end of the room to the other. The dark carpet did not have a speck of dust or dirt, as if it was cleaned daily. All the chairs at the table were leather, and very comfortable. Everyone was on the other side of the boardroom gathering refreshments and speaking amongst themselves.

“This must be important if Matthias is flying in,” the Chief Operations Officer, Jamie Wilson, said as he put some small blocks of cheese on his plate.

“To hop on a flight from Los Angeles seems like it’s something urgent. I’m not really looking forward to seeing what that urgent thing could be,” one of his direct reports, Nicholas, said.

Nicholas was one of the directors over several of the operations teams.

“I should have had a few shots of Tequila before this meeting,” another executive said before walking back to the table.

While most of them stood and talked, a pro basketball game was being shown on the flat screen. Jamie glanced over to the table to see one of the senior directors of finance glued to his laptop and jotting into the notebook that was beside him. The notebook was full of graphing paper and bar graphs. The man worked diligently, going back and forth between writing quickly on his notepad and scattering his fingers across his laptop keyboard.

“Walter,” Jamie calmly called out to him, two small plates in his hand. He did not receive a response. “Walter,” he said a little stronger. “Walter!”

Jamie caused the man to finally look up, drawing the attention of others also. Jamie then walked over and handed him one of the small plates, which had a few blocks of cheese, sausage, and some crackers.

"Take a break. All of this work isn't going anywhere," he said with a grin.

The two of them worked together at Anomaly for almost fifteen years. During those years together, they developed a close friendship.

"You're right," Walter stood up, towering over Jamie with his six-foot five frame. "I need to use the bathroom before this meeting. I appreciate the cheese."

Walter Berry was the Senior Director of Finance and had been for the last five years. He was a tall black man; black hair with grey sprinkled all throughout, fifty-four years old, and had large hands that seemed capable of both crushing boulders but also gliding elegantly across a keyboard. Walter's muscular build and broad shoulders could be quite intimidating. He was an intelligent man and very good with numbers. Walter was a graduate from Toma and was usually one of the smartest in his circles, even amongst some of his Toma peers. Toma was a very prestigious university in New York, it was a very difficult university to get into.

As he walked down the hallway towards the bathroom, he pulled out his cell phone to see text messages from his wife, Laura Berry. He called her instead of texting back.

"Working late I'm guessing?" Laura answered with annoyance in her voice.

"Emergency meeting. Matthias is flying in, I think he landed about twenty minutes or so ago," Walter told her.

"I hope they don't keep you all night!"

"Hopefully not."

Walter stepped into the bathroom. He walked over to the urinal, using his shoulder to hold the phone up to his ear.

"Well since he's in person, we'll hear something about the promotion, right?" Laura asked.

"Hopefully; it's been two weeks so he should have an answer for me. Pray for me," he said.

"Of course. Just hurry home, you know we need to start preparing for the trip next weekend. There's not much we need to do, but there's much we need to do—if that makes sense."

"It doesn't," Walter chuckled, heading to the sink to wash his hands. "Are your parents coming? You never said if they were going to make this trip."

"They're coming, and Katie is too!" Laura said cheerfully, causing Walter to grin at her excitement.

"I cannot tell you how worried I was that she wouldn't, she's bringing Derek with her."

"Derek?" Walter's grin faded as he dried his hands and left the bathroom.

"Her boyfriend. Remember? We have talked about this."

As Laura began to further elaborate, someone stepped in the hallway and signaled for Walter to hurry back.

"We'll talk later, I have to go."

Walter hung up the phone and quickly walked back to the conference room. Before he made it back, a text message from 'Isaac Duke' came to his phone:

What's up old man! I hope all is well. I'll be in Dallas in the next few weeks. I'd love to grab a drink and catch up. Take care and tell the family I said hello! Love you man!

Walter grinned and put his phone back in his pocket. When he stepped back into the conference room, everyone was seated, prepared to lock in and focus. The relaxed and lighthearted atmosphere seemed to be no longer as everyone was ready to get down to business. A hand clamped onto Walter's shoulder. He then felt a pat on the back from that same hand. He turned around to see the CEO Matthias London standing behind him, extending his hand for a handshake. Matthias was a young Caucasian man in his mid-thirties, a head full of jet-black slicked back hair, a sly grin fixed on his face. He shook Walter's hand, proceeding to make his way around the room to greet the others.

Matthias was a very confident man, despite being younger than the majority of those that reported to him. His confidence was often mistaken for arrogance. His father, John London, who was a professor at Toma for some time prior to getting into the business lane, was the founder and original CEO. Toma was a topic that Walter was able to use to build rapport with John. John stepped down and passed the reins of the company to his young hotheaded son Matthias when his family and marriage fell apart due to an affair that went public, accompanied by fraud allegations.

"Thank you for all of your patience," Matthias commenced, pulling off his suit jacket. "If this wasn't of vast importance, I would not have flown here to speak to you."

Some of the members of the e-board despised Matthias but concealed it to the best of their ability. Many of them were envious, feeling that Matthias fast-tracked his way to the top – no hard work, no struggle, nothing to show that he deserved the position that he was in. The swagger with which he carried himself was something that continuously rubbed people the wrong way.

“We have been losing money, and losing it at a very rapid rate,” he said strongly. “Walter brought it to my attention last week. He and his team monitored a few things, and many irregularities were found. I understand that we are in the process of replacing our previous CFO, but this must be addressed. Plain and simple, money is being stolen from us somewhere.”

Matthias then looked down at his watch.

“Not only are we losing money, but also information,” he grabbed the remote to the flat screen and turned to his assistant. “Is this the channel? Is this it?”

She nodded to confirm. Matthias turned the volume up and sat the remote down. The first half of the basketball game had just ended. When the commercial break came, the quick segment that flashed across the screen caused eyes to widen and mouths to drop. The chairman of a business appeared on screen, speaking about a new operating system tool that his company integrated and how pleased he was with it. Several in the boardroom immediately recognized him when he came on the screen. Once the commercial ended, Matthias quickly turned the television off and slammed the remote against the marble table, hand still resting on top of it. His assistant walked over quickly handing him a glass of water.

"Was that what I think it—" one of the execs was interrupted by Matthias throwing his glass at the flat screen, sending fierce, jagged lines across the screen. Silence fell over the room, but no one was caught off guard. Matthias' fits of rage were nothing new to his executive team.

"The project we spent north of four million dollars to initiate, complete, and launch by the end of the year, New Year's Day!" Matthias yelled.

The room remained completely silent. All their meetings for the past six months, all their marketing and everything else centered around the development of their new virtual operating system tool for the business market. Anomaly was an industry leader in new and innovative home and commercial technology but had been playing catch up as of late. The project that would have propelled them ahead was now compromised.

"So…what do we do?" an e-board member broke the silence.

"Our developers are working to see what modifications or other beta models we can implement. We have put too much money into it, so we can at least make it better. In the meantime, talk to no one.

No personal company information should leave this room, laptops from now on don't leave here either," Matthias declared to them.

Everyone in the room clinched their jaws in frustration but held their piece.

"We'll be conducting interviews and network checks over the next few weeks; see where we can close any leaks that we may have. Understand this: if any of you are found questionable or in a compromising position, it will not be pretty."

Not much was stated after that. The meeting was dismissed, and Matthias remained seated at the head of the table. His assistant quickly got on the phone with the building maintenance crew to address the broken flat screen.

"Walter," Matthias called out to him.

Walter looked up to see Matthias motion for him to come to the head of the table. Walter put on his suit jacket, picked up his briefcase, and made his way to the head of the table. He had no intention of speaking privately with Matthias but anticipated hearing some news about possibly being promoted to CFO, which he and others felt he was qualified for.

"My father asks about you all the time. He says that you're a good man. I know you and I have only spoken a few times solely on business, but I just wanted to talk a little bit with you."

"John is a good man," Walter smiled. "I'm thankful for all that he showed me."

"Big plans coming up for the weekend?"

"Not much of anything this weekend, but family time next weekend down in Galveston."

"Excellent, that should be an amazing time," Matthias nodded.

The end of the small talk gave way to an awkward, expectant silence.

"Well, I held you back because I wanted to address something with you. I didn't want you to hear any rumors or chatter; I wanted you to hear it come from me."

"Understood," Walter said.

"As you know, Vaughn has officially stepped down from the role of CFO and we've been piecing it together since. With all that is going on, I must appoint someone sooner rather than later," Matthias said. "I'm going to be appointing Whitney."

Walter remained quiet as Matthias continued to stare directly into his eyes. Whitney Pratt was another director, younger than Walter, located in Anomaly's Boston location. As moments passed, Walter's face reddened almost visibly. He was highly disappointed and became more disappointed as he began to mentally compare his resume and accolades to Whitney's.

"I don't understand," Walter finally said.

"Well, with where we are right now, I think it's best that you're closer to ground zero and to the analysts as well as their managers. You know finance and accounting here has a massive headcount; I need experienced supervision over those managing all those teams. Whitney has a little more of a background better suited for analyzing and resolving at the executive level."

Matthias stood up, not comfortable with the feeling of Walter towering over him.

"But, with all that I've done, I know this company's books inside and out, I'm sure Whitney would be better—"

"Walter," Matthias put his hand up. "The decision has been made."

"Whitney is in Boston. I'm already based here."

"He will be here in Dallas by Wednesday," Matthias began to lose his patience. "Walter, it's done. The announcement will be going out on Monday. I just thought I would give you the respect of telling you before it was announced."

Matthias pat him on the shoulder and began to walk off. Walter gritted his teeth as he became even more upset. He felt like his years of experience and all that he had done in preparation for this possibility was slapped down. Walter still did not know what to say or how to continue the conversation. The entire conversation was made more unbearable by Matthias' lack of empathy.

"I'm going to take some time off this week--prepare for my family coming in town," Walter said strongly.

Matthias stopped and around before exiting the conference room with a slight smirk on his face.

"Take all the time you need."

CHAPTER 2

The setting sun ushered in the night as Walter cruised down the highway, listening to the old school music blaring through the speakers of his black Bentley truck. The cool breeze outside made the drive home that much more therapeutic for him. The conversation he had with Matthias continued to replay in his mind, and the smirk on Matthias' face was an image burned into his mind. Laura called him twice since he last spoke with her, but he did not answer. He turned his radio all the way down as he pulled into the driveway of his beautiful red bricked home, which was at the end of the block where a roundabout was. McKinney, Texas had several nice homes. A white Range Rover truck was parked in front of the three-car garage, the windows were very dark due to the tint on them. The grass was as smooth as carpet and bright green, not a blemish anywhere.

When he walked into the house, the smell of Jambalaya hit his nostrils along with the music playing throughout the house hitting his ears. Polished hardwood floors ran through the living and dining rooms. Everything was brighter toned colors, intensified by the white walls. The numerous family pictures on the living room walls and around the house made the environment that much more welcoming. As he put down his briefcase, his wife emerged from another room, swaying back and forth. She was in an all-white bathrobe, Flexi-rods in her hair, singing the song playing word for word as she stared at Walter.

Laura Berry was six years younger than Walter. Although originally from New Orleans, Louisiana, many of her teenage years were spent in Muskogee, Oklahoma, a place that she left at the age of eighteen and never looked back. Laura never envisioned the life that she lived; she had a much different plan in mind as a young hotheaded teenager. She could not care less about what anyone thought of her, and it often got underneath Walter's skin. She often teased Walter because he was an esteemed, tightly wound man in corporate America while she was the complete opposite, which kept Walter grounded. They were on their twenty-eighth year of marriage. Despite several challenges early on, neither of them wanted to be anywhere else or with anyone else. The two of them struggled early on due to differences in how they saw the world, and a few financial struggles, some of which came from Walter's issues with gambling in his younger years.

“Why didn’t you park in the garage?” Walter asked.

“Nice to see you too,” Laura said, playfully spinning as airily as a ballerina.

They wrapped their arms around each other and began to dance. Laura purposely did not ask about Walter’s bothered expression, hoping to keep the moment going.

“You know what song this is?” Walter asked.

“You had this on repeat that night we sat in your car talking the whole night. Third date, maybe,” she rolled her eyes.

“You fell in love that night,” Walter smirked.

“I was tired and ready to go,” she fired back. “And that restaurant was not all that.”

“You told me it was the most romantic night you ever had,” Walter looked down at her, mildly towering over her.

“Okay well you got me, so there’s that,” she shrugged and walked away.

Laura asked Walter about his meeting at work, then quickly walked into the kitchen. She knew asking work related questions was like opening pandora’s box. Walter went into more depth than Laura asked for just as she expected him to. As Walter explained, she walked back into the family room and stood in front of him, an oven mitt on one hand and a glass of white wine in the other.

"They couldn't have gone over all of that in a conference call?"

Walter's eyes widened and his mouth dropped a little.

"Laura, this is not a joke," Walter said strictly. "This is my career."

"I know," she took a sip of the wine. "I am sorry it didn't go the way you wanted. I— "

"That I wanted?" Walter interrupted her.

"That *we* wanted," she said with an eye-roll. "I know that you—*we*—were looking forward to that promotion. It may not have happened today, but it will happen when it's time."

Laura kept the work talk to a minimum. She was rarely in the mood to hear Walter vent about his work frustrations. Those were conversations that could go on for hours and too much of it would stress her out. Laura worked as a schoolteacher for a few years before and after she and Walter got married, she stopped due to severe battles with stress and anxiety. She used to come home and pour all her frustrations onto Walter, and therefore had a high level of grace for his venting.

Walter glanced down at the table to see an old beat up small blue leather journal with a red ribbon hanging out of it. He picked it up and began to flip through the pages. On the inside, there were poetry lines written in red ink.

"What is this?"

"What's what?" Laura asked, walking back out from the kitchen. "Oh, I'm surprised that was left here. I found it earlier today. You know she used to take it everywhere; she would lose it if anybody touched it."

"Right," Walter said.

He hadn't looked up once, glued to reading the pages. Laura quickly walked over and snatched the small journal out of Walter's hands.

"Invasion of privacy!"

"It was left here, it's probably old," Walter said, reaching for the journal.

"That doesn't mean you can read through it!" Laura slapped Walter's hand away and tucked the journal under her armpit. "What if someone went looking through your mess in that office?"

"You have," Walter said.

"That's not the point," Laura smiled.

"You don't care to read it because she has always been more open with you. It was like pulling teeth for her to talk to me about anything."

Walter reached over the couch to turn on one of the lamps.

"It wasn't always that way," Laura said. "If you really wanted to know what your daughter was thinking, you would have come with us to visit her these past few years. I always told you what would happen when she was younger."

Laura sat across Walter's lap and wrapped her arms around his neck.

"I just wanted the best for her. I was being an active father," Walter said.

"Then what happened?" Laura asked sarcastically. "You call these last few years active?"

"I've reached out. I've called. If she doesn't want to answer and doesn't care to talk, I'm not going to force it. She's grown," Walter said.

"So…you just give up? What good is that going to do?" Laura asked.

"What is this about?" Walter looked at Laura, who frowned at the question.

Laura stood up and crossed her arms.

"This is about the fact that our daughter has not been home in almost five years. I have only been able to see her when the kids and I have gone to North Carolina and you have not seen her since before she moved to New York! That is not normal, and it is not right. I don't see how you can be so comfortable knowing that your daughter has not come back here in so many years."

"Laura…" Walter stood and grabbed Laura's hands gently. "You know work has been very demanding these last few years. But I am excited to see her, her friend too."

Laura became frustrated; it was clear that Walter was purposely deflecting.

"Why do you keep ignoring what I'm saying? This isn't about Derek," Laura said.

The two of them made their way to the bottom of the stairwell, which circled up to the second level of their house.

"Daddy is going to kill him," a small high-pitched voice came from the top of the stairway.

A little girl stood at the top of their stairs. Her hair was a huge poof from being combed out and blow-dried. She had a mischievous grin on her face because she already knew that she was not supposed to eavesdrop on Laura and Walter's conversation.

"Olivia, what did we say about when daddy and I are talking?" Laura asked.

Olivia, their ten-year-old daughter, began to slowly back away from the stairs with a bashful look on her face.

"Oh no, don't back away now miss thing, come here!"

Though Laura's voice was piercing and urgent, she maintained a warm and inviting smile. She glanced over at Walter, who pointed to his head with a look of confusion, referring to Olivia's hair.

"You are more than welcomed to finish dinner or her hair, since you're so observant," Laura said.

Olivia was one that asked many questions and possessed a keenness that seemed beyond her age. She was the spitting image of a younger version of her mother, including Laura's bright hazel eyes. Laura always made sure that she spoke to Olivia and addressed her like a young woman, not a ten-year-old child. She loved her children, and even when she spoke firmly to them, she could not help but to smile and laugh about them. She wasn't strict to the point that they did not enjoy their childhood, which was something she and Walter often butted heads about, especially when it came to their oldest daughter. Before going upstairs, Laura stepped back down the stairs in front of Walter.

"Think about what I said."

Laura kissed him and made her way up the stairs. Walter walked through the family room into a side hallway that led to his office. The back wall was covered up with a large bookshelf full of books. The other walls were covered with framed diplomas and other certificates of accomplishments. His office had a dark tone due to the dark brown wood. It was impeccably clean and perfectly organized. Amid the dark tones were bright and colorful family pictures of him, the children, as well as of Laura. There was one picture of Laura that he loved which rested on his desk. It was a framed black and white candid picture of her, a huge smile on her face, beautiful and radiant. Walter grabbed a cigar out of a wooden box on his desk and cut off the tip before sitting down at his desk, he loved cigars. The sound of someone abruptly coming in front door interrupted the brief silence.

"Jared, I told you to clean up this room and the bathroom!" Laura yelled from upstairs.

Walter glanced towards his office door to see his sixteen-year-old son dart past, running full speed into the kitchen, throwing his keys on the counter.

"Jared," Walter said firmly.

The sound of several things falling over in the kitchen shortly followed. Walter stood up to walk towards the kitchen. Before he could get there, Laura appeared like a flash headed into the kitchen. She snatched Jared by the arm, who began to explain himself and plead with her as to why he was late getting back home. He was supposed to have been home a while ago to do certain chores that Laura had laid out for him. For many, Jared's adorable face made it difficult to be upset with him, but Laura was always able to look right past it. Jared was always the most challenging out of all their kids, the complete opposite of their six-year-old son, Tristan. One of the things that Jared knocked over was the blue journal. Walter grabbed the journal as his cell phone began to vibrate.

"You scared to answer the phone?" his brother Jeffrey's deep voice came across the phone. "I've been calling you for over a week now."

"I've been busy."

Walter went back to his office and sat in his leather chair, cigar in his mouth.

"Busy? You didn't have to relocate your family to another state these past two months," Jeffrey responded.

Jeffrey Berry was his older brother, who lived in Boston with his wife and children. He was an accountant doing very well for himself. Walter was the youngest of three children. His brother Jeffrey was the middle child, and their sister Janice was the oldest.

"Still catching heat about choosing Boston over San Diego?" Walter asked.

"You know I am. You know some black folks don't like Boston unless they're from here—most of us," Jeffrey said, causing both to chuckle.

As they spoke, Walter flipped through his daughter's blue journal that he picked up.

"I got an early copy of Janice's new book; it is incredible," Jeffrey told him.

"Didn't she just release her last one?" Walter asked, quickly agitated. "That one is still making rounds, right?"

"It is, but she said she couldn't wait any longer, so she's putting out another one. She already has a few interviews lined up. Should be airing sometime in the next few weeks."

"Nice, I'll have to text her and congratulate her," Walter said dryly.

"It's crazy how quickly this one is taking off. She's got a lot going—"

"Did you call me to talk about Janice? She talks about herself enough for all of us."

There was a brief pause, and then Jeffrey continued with the conversation.

"I called to tell you that I have heard about what's going on at Anomaly, the money being lost, and the rumored information being leaked. You know Whitney Pratt is based here in Boston, he and some of my colleagues run in the same circles. I heard chatter about him getting promoted earlier this week," Jeffrey grabbed Walter's attention. "I know how much of a perfectionist you are; I just don't want you to let this consume you as you have the last few years."

"Earlier this week?" Walter raised his voice. "And you didn't tell me?"

"I have called a few times," Jeffrey responded. "But honestly, I didn't know how you would take it. So, you know what, I was a little hesitant to be honest."

"I'm doing what every person does to move forward and secure the future—the same thing you do, the same thing Janice and everyone else does."

"Yeah, but you don't have the balance. You have a great life where you are even apart from work. I wouldn't even call this whole situation a setback."

"Easy for you to say, Jeff. This isn't happening to you. Let this have been you or Janice; you wouldn't see it as a simple setback."

He suddenly came across a picture of a couple that was towards the middle of the blue journal. It looked to have been used as a bookmark. The pages were blank after where the picture was. Walter immediately recognized his oldest daughter in the picture as well as the young man. The picture was taken on a bright afternoon. The young man in the photo had his arm around her, giving her a kiss on the cheek. She was looking up. The picture captured what must have been a good bout of laughter. The two of them were dressed formally and made for a beautiful couple. On the back of the picture there were three words written in bright red: *The Family You Choose*.

"You can't compare what you got going on with anybody else, including us. We are not in competition. We're family, so we're supposed to make sure we all make it. The family is more important than all of this."

"You're right Jeffrey. Whatever you say."

CHAPTER 3

Charlotte, NORTH CAROLINA

GRACE GOSPEL CENTER

SUNDAY MORNING

The bright sun shined down beams of light that polished and glistened the cars that packed the parking lot in front of Grace Gospel Center, a church right off the highway just within the city border. The outside looked like a traditional church building of the sixties, giving off a civil rights era feel. The inside had all the modern-day touches and technology that instantly reminded people of the modern day and time. The bright red carpet inside made everything look more vibrant. The diverse congregation, made up of over seven hundred people, clapped and sang along with the praise team on stage leading them in song. The praise team consisted of twenty singers leading the songs, a drummer, a guitarist, a saxophone player, and a young man on the keyboard. Each of them on stage were coordinated as far as wearing red tops and black bottoms. It was difficult for one not to sing and clap along when in the building, one could easily see that much rehearsal and effort was put into the music. At the end of the current song, the team stopped and the young man on the keyboard continued to play. He was very talented, creating unique sounds that were not easy to create. Once he finished, there was a standing ovation and roar from the congregation, applause for him but also shouting praises to God.

"Well, he is on fire today, isn't he?" the pastor, Roy Loren, said into the microphone, causing another roar and applause from the congregation.

As the musicians began to exit the stage while Pastor Loren addressed everyone, the young man that was on the keyboard stared into the crowd. His focus was on someone that sat a few rows back from the front. To him, her face stood out and everything else around her was non-existent. When he made eye contact with her, she quickly looked away, trying to hold back her grin.

"Do you plan on going to take a seat brother Derek?" one of the elders of the church snapped him out of his daydream.

Derek Dupree, the talented musician, stepped off the stage and walked down one of the side aisles. He shook a few hands and waived at some of the members that he knew on his way to the far-right section where the band and the praise team usually sat. They shared bonds that developed through rehearsals, fellowship, and time spent serving. It was not uncommon for laughs, jokes, and conversation to come from their section. Many members, especially the teenagers and other young members, enjoyed sitting close to them for occasional laughs and even gossip. Derek walked through the row, finally reaching a seat. He was a twenty-eight-year-old from Chicago and had been a member of GGC since his sophomore year of college. Derek was six foot two with an athletic build and larger hands than most, which helped him tremendously during his basketball playing days in high school and two years in college. Everyone loved Derek; he was a gentleman and had a warm, welcoming spirit that was topped off by his compelling smile.

As soon as he sat down, he felt his phone vibrate. He received a text message from 'K Beans':

'Well you on fire today aren't you???'

Derek turned around to look at the woman that he focused on from the stage. She purposely tried not to look at him with a smirk on her face. The two of them silently laughed at each other when they finally made eye contact. When Derek turned around to pay attention, two other members of the band shook their heads at him, having been watching him the whole time. Many of the members often stayed around after church to socialize. As Derek walked into the lobby to greet people and shake hands, one of his close friends, Troy Loren, followed behind him.

"Ayo bro," Troy said, tapping him on the shoulder. "Me and Shanice are headed out. You down to hoop later?"

"You actually coming out? Wow!" Derek yelled dramatically, excited.

"Man shut up. Yes, I'm coming out there," Troy said as they laughed. "I'll hit you."

Troy Loren, the pastor's son, was one of Derek's closest friends. They became friends shortly after Derek became a member at GGC when they both were eighteen. Troy also had a younger sister named Joy. Troy and Joy hated that their parents gave them names that rhymed with their father's name, Roy. They all met serving in one of the young adult groups at church.

After weaving through the rest of the crowd and getting closer to the front doors, the woman that Derek watched during church came into view, speaking with someone. She was a beautiful woman with a glow about her that was undeniable. Her bright hazel eyes were first to stand out about her to most people; they were difficult to forget. People also often admired how well she dressed and put herself together. When Derek walked up, she glanced over at him, then quickly turned back to Tasha, the woman that she was speaking to.

"So sometime this week come by," Tasha said to her.

"Okay, probably will be like Wednesday or somewhere around there."

"Perfect. Love you."

The two of them quickly hugged prior to Tasha rushing off. Once Tasha left, the apple of Derek's eye looked down at the small gold watch around her wrist before looking up at him.

"It's about time," she said, hands on her hips.

Derek didn't respond, but instead reached towards her for a hug. She placed her hand on his chest to block his attempt.

"On fire, aren't you?" she asked, causing Derek to chuckle.

"Here you go," he put his arm around her, and they began walked out of the church.

"You always have me out here waiting, trying to talk to everybody. I'm going to start leaving you," she said.

"You look so good today," Derek said, ignoring her comment.

"Ah ah, don't try to butter me up," she playfully hit him, smiling.

"I'm serious, though. I keep looking at you like… man!"

Katherine Berry was Derek's girlfriend. The two of them had been together for a little over two years; but had known each other for ten years. She and Derek first met as young eighteen-year-old freshmen in college. Despite knowing each other all throughout college and being good friends, they both went in separate directions after the first year. They both were very active in school and stayed busy. Derek was always crazy about Katie; she always occupied his thoughts. It was not until some years after college that she was open to explore being more than distant friends, or as Derek liked to put it, 'came to her senses.' Their relationship was a huge highlight in Derek's life; something he thanked God for while at the same time something he could not believe.

Derek opened the driver door of Katie's blue Jeep for her to get in.

"I'm hoopin' later with Troy and them," he told her as she eased into the car.

"I know. I heard his big mouth all the way from where I was. I'm going to be with Bianca later so go do whatever," she pulled at one of the long strands of hair that came from Derek's beard. "Are they going to survive without you next weekend?"

When she said that, Derek's slight smirk turned to a full smile.

"They'll be alright. Man, that time flew. It's almost show time," he rubbed his hands together.

"Show time?" Katie asked, sighing.

"Show time, the kid is meeting the folks for real this time." he said jokingly.

Katie's demeanor changed drastically from a few moments ago when she was in a good mood. She became irritated just bringing it up, which Derek didn't understand.

"Oh, and my Jeep needs to be washed, it's getting a little dirty in here."

"Really though?" Derek frowned. "I feel like I just washed this Jeep."

"That was weeks ago," Katie said with a mischievous grin. "You already know the deal; I don't know why you always put up this fight."

Derek took a deep breath, knowing that he did not have anything to debate. Katie smiled and gave him a quick kiss.

"Alright go on, I'm out."

When she pulled off, Derek stood in the parking lot watching her drive away. A random smile crossed his face. He often thought about the days when it seemed there was no hope for the two of them coming together and compared it to their present situation.

“I love that girl.”

CHAPTER 4

A large high school was up the road from GGC, which was where Derek and a few others played basketball every Sunday. They chose to play there because of the massive field house. Although there was one main basketball court, the field house had five full basketball courts in addition to an indoor track. The field house was empty on Sundays, so they and the others that joined them had it all to themselves, four against four. The last thing one would assume was that their games were meaningless. The intensity these men played with was as if they were playing for more than just bragging rights.

Derek ran down court and let out a scream as he viciously dunked the basketball, causing others on his team to feed into his energy. He was very athletic and stayed in great shape by consistently going to the gym throughout the week. It was a discipline that he developed from playing sports most of his life, which carried over into life after sports. He could play basketball for hours not just due to him being in shape, but also because he loved the game. After the fifth pick-up game, they all sat on the floor against the bleachers, drenched in sweat.

"Derek out there playing like it's the Western Conference Finals," Troy said, causing a few others to laugh and agree.

"Bro out here trying to get a contract," Reggie, one of the others, added through the catching of his breath. "Forget playing the keyboard; we need to get you to a tryout!"

Some of the men were people that Derek and Troy both grew close to at GGC, and they brought others along with them. It was rarely the same faces that came out to play every Sunday.

"Seriously, you got me re-evaluating life. I'm definitely out of shape," Troy told him, which Derek did not want to admit made him feel good about himself.

While Derek was athletic, Troy was not. He was much shorter, and the weight he'd put on caused him to be a little heavier than he was used to.

"Man, man, man," Troy winced as he sat stretching his legs out. "I should not feel this old."

"You gotta' get back in the gym bro, and you been missing for weeks," Derek said as he slipped on his shirt and took off his shoes.

"I've been trying to get back to it." Troy pulled his phone out of his book bag. "Next weekend I'll definitely be back out here if it's a go."

"Y'all will have to set that up; I won't be in town. You know, me and Katie are going on her family trip next weekend."

"Ahh, I see." Troy's eyes widened, and a huge grin crossed his face. "Spending time with the family! You ready for it?"

"I'm ready for it," Derek helped Troy off the floor.

"Is this your first time meeting them?" Troy asked. "Or second time?"

"I met them briefly at graduation. We weren't together then. Her mom came to Charlotte a few times. I didn't see her but maybe once. It wasn't a pressing issue for either of us really. But I've never traveled with them or spent days with them. We don't really talk about it, and she never seems pressed to get me to them, even though she been to Chicago."

He and Derek walked over to the others, shaking hands, exchanging hugs, and saying farewells before walking towards the exit doors. The walk to the exit doors was long due to how large the field house was.

"A lake house trip sounds legit," Troy said, walking with a slight limp due to the soreness in his legs.

Derek did not say anything, causing there to be an awkward silence as they reached the exit doors and made their way into the parking lot.

"I'm just ready for it to be over because by the time it's over, I'll already have their blessing to go ahead and…you know."

Derek nodded to indicate what he was not trying to say aloud. Troy's confusion suddenly turned into a look of surprise as he stopped walking and dropped his bag.

"My dawg!" he yelled and began laughing in excitement. "That's what I'm talking about!"

Troy now seemed to be perfectly fine, no more leisure walking and a new boost of energy from his excitement.

"Relax," Derek said calmly, unable to keep himself from smiling. "Keep that on the low."

"I will bro, relax." Troy stopped walking again.

"That includes Shanice bro." Derek put his hand on Troy's shoulder.

"I can't tell my wife?" Troy's voice raised, still with a fixed grin on his face.

Derek's eyes widened at Troy's question.

"No! You know she has a big mouth. No man, no. You can't tell—"

"Alright! I got you!" Troy yelled, still with a huge smile on his face.

Shanice was Troy's wife, another person that served in some of the young adult groups with Derek, Troy, and Joy at GGC. Shanice was at home seven months pregnant with what would be her and Troy's second child. Derek never knew Shanice to keep a secret or be silent about anything for as long as he'd known her. When people found out some business that they probably should not have, Shanice usually was the source of it.

Derek and Troy reached their cars and after putting their bags in, leaned on their cars to continue the conversation.

"Honestly, I'm not surprised, mainly because of who it is," Troy said to him. "When I used to even say the word 'marriage' to you… boy… you would have a meltdown. It seemed like the thought of it was hell to you."

"It was, with those women. It sounds scary when it is with somebody you really cannot see a future with, or you are trying to force one. Trying to force a future you not all in on is a scary thing."

Troy nodded in agreement.

"I'm happy for you. You have been waiting on this for a long time. We been talking about this girl for years, so you should be ecstatic."

“I’ve been trying not to overthink it. I think the only hurdle I have is dealing with her dad man. I haven’t met him, and I don’t know much about him,” Derek said. “But from what I’ve heard about him in the past, he might give me some hell.”

“Why would he? You are a good dude; I don’t see him having a problem with you. Like you said, don’t overthink the whole thing.”

“I mean, I been with Katie all this time and haven’t talked to him. That might come off the wrong way. He sounds like a no non-sense, cutthroat dude just from some of what I’ve overheard her saying to other people. When I ask about him, she doesn’t really say much—”

“Look,” Troy cut him off. “You are overthinking. If you step to her pops scared and shaky, you think he will feel any more confident about you?”

Troy was wise, and often gave Derek the best advice. Most of his life went against the grain of regular society, and Troy was a person that Derek saw as an example to follow.

“Just don’t think about it right now. That’s what I did to keep it a buck with you.” Troy opened his driver door, revealing a large box of diapers.

Derek’s eyebrows raised when the large box came into view.

"Man, Chad runs through these. I've never seen a baby use the bathroom like he does man," Troy explained.

Chad was his two-year-old son.

"So, what's the plan?"

Derek leaned back against his car and looked up into the sky, visualizing how the trip was going to go in his mind.

"Go on this trip, do my thing, come back, and propose a few days after my birthday. That gives me two months to plan it out completely."

"Dope."

Troy finally got the huge box of diapers into his backseat. He turned around to see Derek randomly smiling.

"What are you smiling about?"

"I just can't believe all of this is going down. I been after this girl for almost ten years, like bro it's really crazy."

"That patience paid off for you."

"I never could see it happening though; plenty of times I was just like forget it, I'm about to do me. I'm still just blown by the whole thing. For the longest, it seemed like I was getting nowhere, now I am sitting up here talking about planning a proposal."

"So, after all that, you almost at the finish line, and you about to let a trip get you tripped up?" Troy asked. "Come on now, we better than that. We ain' scared."

Derek smiled and extended his hand for a handshake, acknowledging that Troy was right.

"Go ahead and make that girl your wife bro, because nothing is out here. Don't hold it up just because you're scared, or you are thinking about what all might go wrong. Go get what's yours."

CHAPTER 5

NAIL SALON.

Charlotte, NORTH CAROLINA

"Ouch!"

"Sorry, so sorry," the nail tech apologized as she continued to cut Katie's toenails.

"Our apologies, she is new," an older man said to Katie as he stood afar, evaluating the nail tech, an Asian woman in her forties.

Katie leaned back in her chair; eyes locked in on the nail tech. The sound of chuckling made her glance over at her cousin Bianca, who held in her laughs as much as she could.

"Are you laughing?"

"Girl, yeah!" Bianca finally let out her laughter.

"She is going a little too hard," Katie leaned over and said as Bianca leaned in towards her.

"I bet, those crusty critters you got," Bianca rolled her eyes.

"Girl shut up," Katie quickly responded.

Bianca Guidry was Katie's first cousin and best friend. The two of them grew up together despite Bianca growing up in New Orleans and Katie growing up in Houston. Katie's mother Laura often traveled to New Orleans to spend time with her sister Mel, Bianca's mother, as well as the rest of their family. Every other summer, Bianca would go to Houston and spend the entire season with Katie; and vice versa. Katie and Bianca traveled to college together and experienced much of their young lives together, as well as learned hard lessons together. She and Katie had similar mannerisms and looked alike in many ways, sharing the same caramel skin complexion, smaller forehead, round nose shape, and smile. Many didn't understand how the two of them weren't sisters. The main difference between the two was that Katie wasn't as petite as Bianca was. Despite the compliments Katie received on the weight that she gained, she wanted to lose a little bit of it and tone up. She often caught them looking at her body and heard their comments, many of which were vulgar or sexual. Bianca dealt with the same experience but on another level. While Katie was a beautiful woman, she was often in the shadow of Bianca. Many men viewed Bianca as flawless, but the beauty was a double-edged sword.

"I swear I'm over these men," Bianca said as she put her phone down.

"What happened?" Katie asked, eyes still fixed on the nail tech.

"The usual, you know. These men just don't know how to date anymore, and this right here," —she held her phone up to show a text thread— "This just reinforces what I been saying. So yesterday, this guy approached me at the listening party I went to… and he's not the most attractive, but since he stepped to me, I decided to at least hear him out."

As she listened to Bianca, Katie could somewhat forget about the discomfort of her pedicure. Bianca's shifting tones, vibrant eyes and passionate gestures always kept people engrossed in her stories.

"So, while he was talking to me…" Bianca's face frowned in disgust and frustration. "I couldn't help but try to keep from throwing up because his breath was so bad. I mean, oh my God, that boy don't brush his teeth?"

"Ooh that's a no-no," Katie said.

"Then he pulled his hat off right," Bianca continued, now burying her face in her palm, causing Katie's eyes to widen with intrigue. "He's balding like crazy in the front, but then has these braids he's holding onto that start like in the middle. I mean, just go ahead and let it go man."

"Why are you talking so bad about this man?" Katie asked.

"Because he thinks that he is that dude. You know I do not talk about people, not for real anyway, but he is so arrogant. I don't know why but I gave him my number. Do not ask me what was going through my head. All he does is text me all day, asking me over and over what I'm doing and what I'm up to! Ask me if he has called me once," she said as Katie continued to laugh. "That's funny yeah?"

Bianca playfully slapped her arm.

"Now that is bad, I feel you. That would annoy me too. I don't even like constantly texting people I actually like." Katie gathered her hair into a ponytail.

"Right! Then he is always trying to get me to come to his house, come to the studio and listen to his whack music. I ain' listening to that trash!" Bianca made Katie burst out laughing.

Bianca gave in and began to laugh also. The nail salon only had a few people in it, so the two of them could speak as loudly as they wanted.

"Take me on a date, call me—like, is all of that dead?"

“You know how these men are love,” Katie said, shaking her head.

“I’m over it. About to drop all of them,” Bianca said. “I swear I’m not shallow, but I might have to give athletes a chance again, and you know how I feel about them.”

When their pedicures were finished, Bianca pulled out her phone and brandished her toes for social media.

“Pedi Sundays!” Bianca then began to make different silly facial expressions before turning her phone towards Katie to record her, who simply threw up the peace sign and grinned.

“What up, what up!” Katie flashed a kiddish grin before just as quickly reverting to a straight face.

“She swears she cool,” Bianca chuckled as Katie playfully pushed her.

As the two of them made their way out, they continued to laugh and joke. Despite living together, it was not uncommon for them to go days without seeing one another. Bianca traveled quite often being a flight attendant as well as taking on small acting jobs from time to time. She was into theater and wanted to act, so she often hunted for auditions and worked on independent projects. Katie was occupied enough with her job and other ambitions. She majored in finance in college, which eventually led to her job as a commercial financial analyst. Although she was good with numbers and her job paid well, it was not something she cared to do. Katie loved to write and was very good with words, which opened the door to opportunities in New York after college. While in New York, she worked for a few well-known publications, met a lot of writers and editors, and received so much inspiration before moving back to Charlotte.

"I need to do like you – go to church and find me a man," Bianca interrupted Katie's thoughts.

"I did not find him at church," Katie said as she rolled her eyes. "We all went to school together!"

"Oh yeah I keep forgetting Derek went to school with us," Bianca laughed at herself. "Girl why I keep telling people you found that boy at church?"

"I don't know, but you need to stop. Y'all got into it for a brief minute back in school, remember?"

"I do remember now that you say it. He is so lame," Bianca sat back in the passenger seat and put her shades on.

"Shut up, y'all were being petty," Katie said. "I hate that you can't come on the lake house trip, especially since we haven't gone in such a long time. You really can't get off work?"

"Girl no, I've switched my schedule up too much so I don't have a lot of wiggle room. I got called in for some auditions that weekend too, so I can't miss that. My mama has already been on me about it. I'm surprised you are going, to tell you the truth."

Bianca lifted her shades and glanced over at Katie.

"I know, but you know how important family is to us so I can only stay away for so long. I just don't know what to expect, not trying to have a weekend full of family drama."

Bianca was upset that she would not be able to make the trip. She, like the rest of their family, valued time spent together. It had been a while since all of them had come together. Katie slammed her horn, screaming at a car that abruptly pulled in front of her.

"You'll have your man to keep you company," Bianca responded. "Is he excited to go?"

"Stupid," Katie said, staring down the driver as she passed by. "But yes, he seems like he is a little more excited than I am."

"You think he's going to pop the question?" Bianca quickly asked.

"On the trip? I would hope he wouldn't do it there of all places. But when we get back, who knows."

"Maybe he wants the family around, you just never know," Bianca said.

"I get it…but not there. To be real with you, I used to be scared that he was going to ask me after like six months," Katie said, swerving back and forth between lanes.

Anyone else would have been hyperventilating, but Bianca, too used to her cousin's driving, didn't flinch once.

"What made you think that?" Bianca asked, looking over her shoulder at the blur of cars they were zipping past.

"Derek has wanted me since we met and has always tried to keep himself in the picture. We have always been just friends. Once we started dating, I got worried that he was going to try to get serious right away."

Katie pulled into their apartment complex, a nice upscale place not far from downtown which wasn't five years old yet.

"Why didn't you just date him back in school? Why did you wait so many years later?" Bianca asked.

"I mean," Katie winced, "I was young; I was too caught up on the situation from high school. Then of course, I was with you know who, and that wore me out. But it wasn't like I didn't know that Derek was somebody I should have been giving my time to. I just felt I was not the type of girl he was going to be expecting, then I thought we would not mesh, it was just a lot. But I had to be honest with myself and realize what was right for me. And here we are."

"You really are in it for love then," Bianca said as they got out of the Jeep and began walking into their building.

There was an uncomfortable moment of silence as they walked. Katie's look of confusion as they walked up the stairs was something Bianca could feel despite not being able to see it.

"Why else would I be in it?" Katie asked.

Bianca glanced back at Katie and frowned at her.

"Derek is cool. Seems like a real nice guy. It surely seems like he makes you happy. But think about security and stability too; it's not all about love all the time. It's not about that at all most times."

Bianca opened the apartment door and threw her hands up after they walked in.

"Lord! Feels so good in here," she sighed, collapsing onto the couch.

The apartment maintained a consistent chill due to the air conditioning never being turned off. Both Katie and Bianca loved keeping the apartment being just above cold. Katie stood behind the island of the kitchen, sifting through a pile of the unopened mail that had built up over the last few weeks.

“So that’s what you are looking for?” Katie asked, still looking down at the mail in her hand.

“It’s what all of us should be,” Bianca quickly turned to face Katie. “I’m not saying that you can’t grow to love the person, but it should be a good move to keep you secure for the future.”

“You sound like you just chasing the bag though, gold digging,” Katie finally said, now looking at Bianca. “Getting with somebody just because of what they can do for you or because they got money?”

“No, I do not!” Bianca fired back, her face twisted with a look of disgust and offense. “That’s not gold digging. People try to act like commitment is all about you loving somebody, and it’s not. People break up all the time over money issues. If love is all you need, then why didn’t it keep them together? Why are we always expected to sacrifice our stability to trust a man’s potential? If we’re trusting potential, we might as well let that potential play out before we put ourselves into it. That’s what I’m doing – not stressing myself out over these men who have nothing for me.”

Bianca loved to debate; she could be very combative when provoked. While Katie had no problem speaking her mind, she was not one that enjoyed going back and forth with anyone.

"It's not that cut and dry at all; you crazy being with somebody you don't love just because it's a stable situation. That's how you end up miserable," Katie responded. "I'm not saying security not important, but I don't think that by itself is enough."

"Look at your parents," Bianca said. "That's what auntie Laura did: she found somebody that could provide security and stability. Look at your dad, and you and everybody else turned out okay because of it."

"Chile' that's a horrible example," Katie said strongly. "Horrible, and you know that's not a good example. The worst one. They have had tons of problems, and because of him."

"No, you just don't want to admit it or give him credit, that's all that it is. The facts are the facts. But gon' and be naïve if you want, I'm just telling you to think and open your eyes. We are not the older generation; things are different now and you already know that. Love alone will have you out here looking stupid. These men are all for themselves."

Bianca was so into getting her point across, she hadn't realized that Katie had already mentally checked out of the conversation. Katie had the habit of internalizing everything and taking words to heart, and Bianca's way of speaking her mind raw and unfiltered often caused uncomfortable conversations between the two of them. Katie went into her room and laid on her bed.

I'm not naive. Love is enough, she thought to herself. *Right?*

CHAPTER 6

MONDAY MORNING.

Charlotte, NORTH CAROLINA

As if being just being Monday wasn't enough, the day made itself tedious with the heaviness of gloomy clouds and a thick shower of rain across the city. When Derek's alarm began to go off at 6am, he simply rolled over and knocked his phone off the nightstand. Being on the phone with Katie late the night before made it more difficult to get out of bed. They did not live together and made a point not to spend a lot of time together late at night by themselves. They mutually agreed to be abstinent and being apart late at night made it easier to do so. Derek lived in a one-bedroom apartment on the outskirts of the city. His apartment was bland, lacking any interesting colors or decorations, apart from a few framed posters of basketball players and some historical activists.

After rolling out of bed, Derek walked around his apartment opening the blinds. He moved quickly due to the cold air gripping his skin, much of which was out since he was wearing only boxers. It generally took him an hour or so to get dressed and be on his way to his job, which was a long drive. Derek needed the long drive to get his mind right and prepare to put his best attitude forth. It wasn't just the thought of work in the morning that impacted his attitude, but also the frustrating reminder of his expensive car note every time he drove. Derek only had his car for four months and had severe buyer's remorse. When he saw others driving newer cars, making moves, he felt that he needed to make a move to at least feel that he was making strides in life. It proved to be one of the worst decisions as the cost of it was too much to keep up.

When he pulled into the parking deck of his job, he could feel his attitude shift and frustration begin to set in. The smell of coffee hit his nostrils as soon as he stepped into the office, which was quiet for eight in the morning. The cubicles were tall enough for everyone to have more than enough privacy in their workspace.

"Good, you're here," a deep monotone voice said.

Derek turned to see his manager Chuck walking towards him with a few documents in his hand. Chuck was a taller black man in his fifties, bald on top of his head with grey and black hair on the sides of his head. What was most noticeable was that his large stomach hung heavily over his waistline.

"Step into my office, young sir."

Chuck walked past Derek, who frowned behind Chuck's back as he followed him into his office. When the two of them sat down, Chuck read and responded to emails as if Derek wasn't there; it was a part of his characteristic condescending behavior. Derek sat slouched in his chair, waiting for Chuck to address him. Chuck kept his office light off; the light that blasted through the window—which was essentially the entire back wall—gave a natural light that cancelled out the darkness. The only sound in the office was Chuck's heavy breathing and the heavy-handed jots he made on his computer keyboard.

"Alright," Chuck sighed heavily and sat the two papers in his hand on front of Derek.

The two papers were reports, one of the pages was festive with graphs and charts while the other was several different paragraphs with reviews and feedback. At the top of both papers was in small bold black letters: DUPREE_D.

"Tell me what's going on," Chuck said.

His tone was grave, but his face showed no real care for the matter.

"What's the problem?" Derek asked, staring at both reports in confusion.

Chuck slowly ran his hand from his forehead down and then crossed his arms, as if extending the last of his patience.

"You mean to tell me you don't see anything wrong with these reports and surveys that we've received on you in the last few weeks?"

"No, I really don't," Derek said, sitting up in his chair.

Derek was fully prepared to leave; he'd reached his breaking point with his job some time ago. While he was grateful to have a job, he was also just waiting for the perfect moment—or excuse—to make an exit. Derek worked for an information security and surveillance company. He was an on-boarding consultant, responsible for traveling to the sites of new clients and walking them through the on-boarding process that the company put together to ensure that their transition was smooth and seamless. The traveling component of the job was one that Derek loved; it was something that made the job tolerable.

"Derek, I'm not going to sugarcoat it. The surveys and feedback we have been getting have not been acceptable. New clients have already been submitting some complaints and rating their on-board experience as ineffective. This has been a trend the last few months. So again, tell me what is happening here."

Derek continued to glance back and forth between Chuck and the reports.

"I don't understand. I make sure I cover every area when I speak to these clients. I go through everything slowly and make sure I address any questions before I leave. I follow up, troubleshoot anything that may happen in the early months, all of that," Derek responded. "When I'm on client sites, they all seem receptive and understand what is going on. If there are more errors, why don't they go to quality control?"

"QC brought it to our attention, some of the issues these new clients are having should be addressed in the on-boarding process," Chuck said strongly. "This was not happening before, and that is what I want you to address. Something has changed, that is undeniable."

"I honestly don't know what to tell you. I come in; I work; I don't play around. When I travel, I practically hold these new clients' hands through the process. I'm here solely to get this work done."

Derek's sincere tone came not from passion, but from the need to keep his job. Chuck sighed again, looking off into space searching for the words to say. There was another awkward silence between them.

Derek glanced out of the office door to see a few of his coworkers attempting to eavesdrop. All of them began making goofy facial expressions, causing Derek to crack a smile. They all immediately scattered when Chuck turned and looked at them. Derek enjoyed most of his coworkers; they were a big help in getting him through the workday.

"You're going under management advisory," Chuck made him snap back to attention.

Derek's smile quickly faded.

"If the feedback and surveys we receive at the end of this month aren't up to par, you know under management advisory you will be asked to leave the company."

Chuck, with movements rehearsed and barely conscious, signed some new documents, then slid them across the desk for Derek for sign. He continued to talk about how he did not want to see Derek fail, but he sounded like paragraphs from the corporate textbook that had no real meaning to Derek. Derek signed the documents while ignoring Chuck altogether. When he finally got to his desk to set up for the day, his phone had several unread messages that distracted him. All the messages were from a group message text thread. The conversation started with a lot of jokes and small talk and led to them all of them agreeing to meet up that evening, awaiting

Derek's response. One of Derek's friends, Anthony Kofi, got a position as a strength and conditioning coach for a I-AA college football program. Before Derek could respond to the text, he glanced up to see a woman staring at him, her head just making it over the top of his cubicle wall. She was a few years older than Derek, white, her brownish blonde hair was in a bun, and round wire framed glasses rested on her face.

"Carey, I swear you could be a serial killer if you wanted to be. I told you about sneaking up on me," he said to her.

Carey, one of Derek's teammates, came from around the cubicle wall and sat on Derek's desk.

"What was he getting on you about?"

"You already know," he shook his head and turned to his computer screen.

"Management advisory?" she asked, looking down and fidgeting her feet with each other.

Derek nodded, pulling off his purple and grey sweatshirt from college.

"You've got to be kidding me," Carey said quietly. "He's so full of it, like so full of it. Let me know if I can do anything to help you; management advisory can be a pain."

"I appreciate that," Derek said to her.

"What are you doing this weekend? Any plans?" Carey asked.

"It's only Monday," Derek said. "I haven't even thought about the weekend."

"You hanging with your girlfriend? How are you guys? It seems like I never hear about her anymore," Carey continued.

"We're good."

Derek pulled out his cell phone and held it low beside his leg.

"So, what are you guys— "

"I need to get this," he interrupted her as his desk phone began to ring.

Derek then quickly put on his headset as Carey began to walk away. Once she was out of sight, the desk phone stopped ringing. Derek put his cell phone on his desk. He called his desk phone from his cell phone to have a reason to end the conversation with Carey. She was one that was not afraid to ask anyone anything, but she proved to be overly intrusive often. Derek's little motivation to do anything was completely gone after his meeting with Chuck. He wasn't in the best position to walk off a job. Derek had to do all that he could financially just to stay afloat. He sat at his desk on his cell phone, responding to the group messages that were coming in. The latest message was one he felt didn't apply to him at all:

So glad all my brothers are doing well in life... We on our way!

CHAPTER 7

McKinney, TEXAS

The BERRY Residence

Silence was something that took Laura a while to adjust to. She was accustomed to the hyperactivity of Olivia and Tristan, but the house was always silent when the children were at school. The sun brightened the entire house, beaming through the windows as Laura straightened up the living room, preparing to leave for the day. Apart from running a bakery with one of her close friends, she didn't punch in a clock anywhere. When Laura stopped teaching, she and Walter agreed it would best for her to be home with their young children as they grew up. Jared and Olivia were homeschooled for a brief period, but that ended when Laura began to have health issues. The current school year was Olivia and Tristan's second year at an actual school.

As Laura walked past the windows that gave view to the backyard, she quickly stopped and walked back to one of the windows. She watched as Walter sat outside in the backyard on one of their wooden yard chairs, dressed comfortably with his feet kicked up as he read a book. Laura quickly walked outside. The sound of her heeled boots caused Walter to turn around and pull his glasses off. Walter analyzed her from head to toe; Laura was dressed in all black with a thick gold necklace around her neck and a gold bracelet around her wrist. She did not have on much make up and her hair was up in a bun. Her sleeveless blouse revealed the tattoo of a long-stemmed rose that began on her wrist and wrapped around her forearm.

"The Lord is good," he said, staring at Laura.

"Why aren't you at work?" she asked, ignoring Walter's compliment. "It's Monday morning."

"I'm just stepping away for a little while, clearing my head," he said with a flirtatious grin still on his face.

"You didn't tell me you were taking time off," she went and sat next to Walter. "Where did you go this morning when you left?"

"I went to the gym for a little bit," Walter said, putting his arm around her.

"Ooh yes," Laura grinned and tapped Walter's stomach, causing him to frown.

"Let's fly down to Florida for a few days, get away from here," he said as he rested his head on her shoulder.

Laura always had an amazing aroma; it was something that stood out about her with everyone. Her scent lingered and drew people, which is often why Walter found himself laying on her or leaning his head on her shoulder.

"We will have enough of a getaway this weekend in Galveston; that will be right on time," Laura said as she delicately rubbed the top of Walter's head. "Are you off the whole week?"

"I am."

"This is not like you. Time off, gym, now talking about a vacation for you and me? I could get used to this," Laura smiled.

"I'm taking a different approach to things these days." Walter stood up. "Maybe good comes to those who rest."

Laura was just excited to have him home. It was rare for the two of them to have time together by themselves. Whether it was work or their children, other things always often pulled their attention and energy away from one another. She stood up along with him.

"You can't work yourself to death," she said as she put her arms around his neck. "Wouldn't you rather spend some time with me?"

"You're right," he said, causing her to smile even more. "Look where working every day and giving my all has gotten me, right?"

Laura's smile immediately faded; she hung her head in disbelief.

"You are not serious right now."

"Very. Why keep spinning my wheels and giving my everything just to get my face spat in?"

Laura then removed her arms from around his neck and stepped back from him. The look of frustration on her face made it clear that she was upset. Before speaking, she took a deep breath to calm herself down.

"You have not stopped talking about this since it happened. It's an obsession at this point. I can't even lay in the bed with you because I know your mind is only stuck on this. You didn't get promoted. It's life, it happens. Life goes on, but you just continue to put yourself through the torture of it."

"It's life?" Walter asked, slighted by how those words casually rolled off Laura's tongue.

"Yes JR, it's life. What more do you want? You have everything, yet you're bent out of shape because you didn't get a position."

"You think this is all about not getting a position? It's more than that!" Walter yelled.

Walter began to feel the same way he felt after leaving Matthias' office, the same wave of emotion began to come over him. Laura's compassion began to overtake her frustration.

"I just don't understand what more you want. We have everything that we could ever need. We have a nice house, money, our kids are taken care of, and we are not struggling anymore. I have never seen you as troubled by something as I have seen you from this, just help me understand it."

Walter took time to gather his thoughts. He knew that if he spoke too hastily, his words would come out wrong and come out emotionally charged. The whole back yard suddenly became bright with sunlight again as the few clouds in the sky moved from covering the sun.

"I went to school, got a degree, and got my masters. I got into the corporate world, spent twenty-three years working and navigating through the system, building up all of the experience that I have."

As Walter spoke, filtering through his frustration didn't stop a brief smile that reflected how proud he was. Laura's eyes were locked on him, genuinely trying to understand and make sense of it.

"Tons of people try to get into Anomaly or a company like it. They couldn't do it. But I did, one of few black people at that time. I put years in there, went above and beyond. I did more to keep Anomaly efficient financially than anyone else has ever done, even though my pay and acknowledgment has rarely reflected it. I have managed hundreds of people. Matt, a young kid not far removed from college, fresh from an office job, already in a well-off situation, gets handed the keys to a multi-billion-dollar company. Just like that," Walter snapped his fingers. "He turns around and spits in my face by promoting someone with less experience and skills than I have. No due diligence, no evaluation – he just moves him up because of the familiarity."

Walter then stopped pacing around and walked back over to Laura, face-to-face with her.

"It's not just about getting a seat at the table; it's how. Despite all that I have done, everything I have put in, I was overlooked and with ease. My qualifications meant nothing. John handed his son the keys and changed his life, not that he wasn't already well off. It is just a constant reminder; I am in no position to give any of my kids that kind of power. I'm not at the top of the food chain where I can just give them the keys to be set for life. That is what drives me, being stuck as a work horse in corporate America and not eating from the ultimate fruit of my labor. Everything we preach to people telling them to do to make it just seems like a lie at times. It's about the big picture."

Walter then kissed her on the forehead before making his way back towards the house, leaving her where she stood. As much as Laura looked for a response, she was not able to find one. She just wanted Walter to be happy at the end of the day, hoping that the upcoming getaway would take his mind off everything. Laura was more worried about how Walter's current state of mind would affect his interaction with their daughter coming, who could be just as strong willed…

CHAPTER 8

Charlotte, NORTH CAROLINA.

Katie's laughter echoed through the car speakers as Derek sifted through the afternoon after-work traffic. The phone call came through Derek's car radio, which made it easier for him to drive, one of the features of his car that he enjoyed. During his drive from work, Derek filled Katie in on the conversation that he had with his manager Chuck. Katie was amused by Derek's description of the conversation, and him venting his frustrations about the job.

"Didn't you say weeks ago that you have been applying for other jobs while at work?" Katie asked him.

"That's not the point though. I still do my job and at a high level," Derek said to her.

"I highly doubt it," Katie laughed with a jovial skepticism.

It was easy for Derek to be open and transparent with Katie, something that he had never felt comfortable doing with other women from his past. In past relationships, Derek would often move as if he was single despite being with someone. When it came to Katie, he wanted to include her and make her a part of his life decisions. Katie often kept a calm disposition and knew how not to make a person feel low, which was what made it easy for Derek and many others to open to her.

"I'm sure we can find something if it comes down to it. Well, it is pretty much down to it now. I'm not worried about it, you shouldn't be either," she told him. "You will have a lot of job transitions in life. It is what it is."

"You are a real one," Derek told her. "That really just made me feel better."

"Always been a real one, don't ever forget it," she spoke over several other women talking in the background. "Where are you going again?"

"I'm meeting up with the crew," Derek told her.

"The crew!" she yelled sarcastically. "Haven't heard about them in a while."

"Don't be like that," Derek said.

"I didn't say anything," she said.

"Uh-huh," Derek sighed.

"I was just saying I hadn't heard about them in a while, that's all I said."

"Yeah okay," Derek said, turning onto his exit. "I thought you would be off by now; why are you still at work?

"I'm not at work. I left early to drive to the school, remember? Ms. Joyce had a few journalism students that I needed to meet."

"That's right, you did tell me that last night. Y'all are working on—" Derek quickly slammed on the breaks and blew his horn at a car that cut in front of him, shaking his head with a scowl on his face. "Ole' dumb… my bad."

Derek caught himself as Katie began chuckling over the phone.

"Don't backslide now," she said. "You sound like me driving."

"People can't drive. I'll let you go, do your thing. I'm about to pull up to Bowe's anyway."

"Alright, I love you," Katie said before getting off the phone.

The conversation with Katie made him feel better about his day. The test now would be if that good feeling would be enough to carry him through time spent with his close friends, who all were moving forward in life while he seemed to be at a standstill.

CHAPTER 9

DARCY UNIVERSITY

Charlotte, NORTH CAROLINA

Darcy was a highly esteemed historically black university that was on the outside of Charlotte. The school was formerly three small separate institutions, but eventually merged into one massive university in 1977. Visitors of the campus were often mesmerized by the large open fields of bright green grass, the towering trees that were covered in spray paint from different fraternities, sororities, and other organizations on the campus, in addition to the numerous dorm and academic buildings. The campus was always busy; some would describe it almost as a small city within itself with how many people moved around and went from place to place when school was in.

Katie and a few others were in one of the many media buildings, which housed the school's radio station, production rooms, and theater stages. She sat at the head of the table in a large conference room; feet propped up on the table revealing the black combat boots that she had on her feet. She also had a baseball cap on her head pulled down low shadowing her face, a purple Darcy t-shirt on covered by her army fatigue jacket. Katie was very comfortable and laid back as she sat scrolling on her cell phone.

"So, when are we trying to launch this?" a voice made Katie suddenly look up.

The question came from a young woman named Sam sitting at the table, accompanied by a few others. Sam, a senior at Darcy, had a pen in hand and a notebook in front of her.

"The goal is to have some traction by this time next year," Katie said, still looking down at her cell phone. "Sorry y'all, I haven't been on social media in forever."

Katie had over twenty thousand people following her social media page, which was something that often blew some of her friends' minds. She tossed her phone onto the table and stood.

"Okay, I'm focused. We're going to do these power hours to brainstorm and shape the vision and the content. It's just easy to focus if we actually meet up and block the time out; life happens, things come up, you know how it goes," she explained to them. "Time to put that Darcy education to work."

"Yeah, as long as these recruiters understand how good a Darcy education is," Sam rolled her eyes.

“Right!” Jade, another Darcy senior student cosigned.

“What do you mean?” Katie asked, crossing her arms.

“I get so tired of answering the same questions; ‘Where is Darcy?’, ‘Is that a university?’, ‘Where is that?’ Like, I want to scream!” Sam yelled, causing the room to laugh. “Put some respect on my school’s name!”

“Get used to that,” Miah Yancey, one of Katie’s friends, chimed in.

Katie had a vision to create her own publication as well as start her own publishing company. Even while she wrote for a major publication when in New York, she always had her own vision and wanted to put her energy into that. Her goal was to create a publishing company that placed more spotlight on the experiences and thoughts of women all around the world and share their stories. The team she assembled was one that she had in mind long before she moved back to Charlotte. Miah went to Darcy with Katie; she wanted to be a part of the team and was a great writer herself. The two seniors, Jade and Sam, connected with Katie while she lived in New York. Once Katie moved back, she reached out to them as promised. Karen Joyce, one of Katie’s old professors, was the one to connect the two of them with Katie.

Ms. Joyce was supportive of Katie and loved her like a daughter.

They sat in the writers' room talking and bouncing different material off one another. Katie was so engaged in the discussion that she ignored her phone vibrating across the table.

"Katie, that's your phone," Jade pointed.

"Who is it?" Katie asked, still not looking at it.

"It's just purple hearts."

When Jade mentioned the purple hearts, Katie quickly walked over to grab her phone. Shortly after she answered, the sound of her mother Laura's voice made her smile. Katie stepped outside to get better reception.

"I am so excited to see you this weekend. You haven't been home in so long," Laura said after their few minutes of small talk.

"I am too, I need a vacation and I miss the kiddos," Katie said.

"They miss you also…you know your daddy misses you too," Laura said.

Katie remained silent for a second, not sure what to say to the comment.

"Is Derek excited?" Laura then asked, breaking the silence. "We are excited to have him."

"He is, he needs a getaway too. It will be good for him to get away from everything. He seems more excited than I am."

"Is he alright?" Laura asked.

The tone of Katie's voice was what made Laura ask. She was very in tune with her children, and although Katie was far away, she could read her easily. Katie began to discuss Derek and some of the struggles that he was having at his job.

"He'll figure it out. He is still young. Just keep being there for him," Laura told her.

"You are always so optimistic," Katie said. "I need to get like you."

"That's what I'm here for, and you are. Girl you're a little me." Laura made Katie grin.

"What is dad doing?" Katie pushed herself to ask.

"He's right here," Laura lowered her voice a little. "We're about to drink some wine and watch whatever this is on the tv, well he has already started."

"He's not working?" Katie asked, surprised.

"He's taking some time off," Laura said.

"You don't sound too excited about it; I thought you would be more relieved," Katie said.

There was another awkward pause between the two of them, the longer the pause, the more Katie began to frown her face.

"Well, I didn't want much. I'm going to let you go, I love you," Laura told her.

As they finished up on the phone, Miah walked out of the building putting her purse over her shoulder. Miah was gracious and gentle whenever she entered someone's space, sweet but nowhere near passive. She and Katie were roommates their first year at Darcy. Despite the two of them being close, their communication was bleak when Katie moved to New York. It became more consistent once Katie moved back to Charlotte.

"Heading home?"

"Yeah girl, I'm tired." Miah gave Katie a long hug. "I have to go pick up Deron from my aunt Lily's house."

Deron was Miah's eight-year-old son.

"Thank you for coming girl." Katie crossed her arms as a cool breeze came through. "Sorry for being on the phone at the end; it was my mom."

"Girl of course, always make some time for Miss Laura. We came up with some good stuff in there so… I'm excited. This got me out of the house for a while, I needed it," Miah said.

"We all need to get together and catch up! Like brunch or something," Katie said in excitement. "Sabrina, Paris, and Imani will all be in town next week for Imani's art show."

Miah's smile began to fade.

"If you want to do a you-and-me thing, I'm down. Otherwise, I'll let you and them have it," Miah said. "I don't really care to be a part of the bourgeois brunch club."

"Don't be like that. We all used to roll together…everywhere," Katie said.

"Yeah, we did," Miah nodded, beginning to reminisce. "But that was then. I started to fall back then when I started noticing things. You didn't notice because you had a life, they didn't. I really was done with them once they started to treat me funny after I got pregnant with Deron. I mean it's all good, I'm not pressed about it. Sometimes you outgrow people, everyone has groups of friends that they don't mix up. I'm just on a different end of the spectrum than they are."

"You know it's not like that Miah. It's life, people have kids."

Katie felt a little uneasy about Miah's comments, mainly because the women she was referring to were women that Katie considered as friends she would have for life.

"I'm not losing sleep over it. I'm just telling you I know what type of women they are. I'm not telling you to drop them or to choose between me and them, you just need to be mindful about how they are. You're nothing like them, that's why you called me to be a part of this and not them but that's another message for another day."

Miah smiled again as Katie rolled her eyes.

"How are you and Derek? I've been meaning to say girl it's about time!" Miah made them both laugh and loosen back up.

"We are good. We're going on a trip this weekend."

"I'm glad he finally got his chance," Miah put her hands together as if praying.

"Yeah, it was overdue honestly, me playing around," Katie said.

She then began to blush as Miah stared at her continuing to smile.

"Aww, I'm so excited for y'all," Miah said. "He has been in love with you forever!"

"Girl go get your son!" Katie said with a laugh.

"I'm gone!" Miah laughed and headed towards her car.

As Katie walked back into the media building, she simply smiled to herself. *Hopefully that love keeps lasting forever.*

CHAPTER 10

McKinney, TEXAS.

The BERRY Residence

The seventy-inch flat-screen lit up the entire living room, the surround sound system made a person feel as if they were inside of the television. Walter sat on the couch with his third glass of wine in one hand and the book that he was glancing through in the other hand. Tristan and Olivia were upstairs; they had an hour or so before Laura was going to put them to bed. Jared was in his room playing video games with one of his friends that lived two houses down. Laura walked over from the piano where she sat their last bottle of wine and laid beside Walter, laying her head on his chest.

"What were you two talking about?" Walter asked.

"Nothing, you know your daughter; not the most talkative," Laura said. "She is excited about this weekend."

"That's surprising," Walter said.

As Laura stared at the TV, she could feel that Walter had more to say. She knew him too well to expect anything else.

"How is her new boyfriend doing?" Walter asked dryly.

"New?"

Laura let out a deep sigh while still staring at the TV, then sat up and looked Walter directly in his face.

"I already know you were listening, say what you have to say. I hate it when you do that."

"I just caught the part where he is having job problems? Again? He can't maintain a job?" Walter asked.

"He's considering other options. People do it all the time. It has nothing to do with maintaining," Laura got up and went straight towards the wine bottle to pour another glass.

"Last time I heard about him he was considering options."

"What's your point?" Laura asked, her annoyance was obvious.

"My point is, why can't he maintain some stability? Where's his drive? He's always starting over," Walter drank the rest of the wine in his glass.

Laura, now with a full glass in her hand, leaned against the piano.

"What does that have to do with anything? We don't know what his situation is or what is going on. Katie wouldn't be with him if he had no drive or ambition about himself."

"And you're sure about that? Because she has changed a bit herself."

"JR, we have talked about this time and time again; Katie is a grown woman more than capable of making her own decisions. How long did it take you to get to where you are now? Were we good in our twenties? Was everything like it is now?"

"I hear you," Walter stood up. "But ever since she got into this relationship, she is not as focused or driven. She just blows in the wind now. She was doing fine when she was in New York. I didn't agree with the move but at least she had some consistency, doing something productive. Now, she moves back for him and doesn't know what she is doing," Walter said to her.

"My God, would you stop? Like please! Who said she moved back for him? Maybe she just wanted to move back for herself?"

The easy flow of these questions, Laura surmised, meant that Walter held those thoughts in for quite some time.

"I didn't raise her to drag a man along with her. She needs someone who can better her, and make sure she is secured in everything. But you know, you all assume I'm just trying to be hard on her," Walter said as he walked towards the kitchen.

"You mean she needs somebody like Isaac, right?"

Walter froze, turning back around to face Laura.

"What is that supposed to mean?"

"I'm not stupid. I see when his name comes across your phone. You wanted Isaac to be your son in law. It baffles me that you even still communicate with him at all, but then again, he boosts your ego. He always acted like you were the best thing since sliced bread. This has nothing to do with Katie being unfocused or whatever BS you are trying to come up with. This is all about her not doing things your way."

Walter didn't respond. He was not about to go back and forth with Laura. He already was not having the best week, and he didn't really want to go to bed to a cold shoulder later. Laura didn't say anything more; she wasn't one to argue but often her anger could be felt through how silent she would be when she was angry. Her silence had the ability to make the entire house uncomfortable. Before either of them said anything else, the rumbling sound of someone running down the stairs broke the silence. Their six-year-old son Tristan came around the corner.

“You almost ready for bed baby?” Laura asked him, her compassionate motherly voice returned as if flipped by a switch.

“Can I have some ice cream?” Tristan pleaded.

“No, it’s too late for ice cream, come on.” She grabbed his hand as they began to walk towards the stairs.

Before being out of sight, Laura turned and gave Walter a scolding stare. She didn’t for a second want him to believe that he was off the hook. Walter sat back down on the couch and made himself comfortable. He was quite confident that he would be sleeping there that night.

CHAPTER 11

Charlotte, NORTH CAROLINA

Bowe's Smoke Room.

Derek's face ached from laughing so much, something he hadn't done in a while. There was much joy and humor in being with his friends, friends that he considered his brothers. All of them met at a small restaurant whose main attraction was the cigar bar and smoke room.

"We had some crazy times man," Elliot Reid, one of Derek's friends, said.

Elliot 'Elle' Reid, Anthony 'Tone' Kofi, and Preston Logan were three men that Derek went through many different life experiences with, his close friends since his first year of college. All four of them were a part of a much larger circle, but the four of them were closest to one another.

"My boy Tone is about to be training college athletes, getting them to the league," Derek said before exchanging an echoing handshake with Tone.

Tone was a heavyset, dark-skinned, muscular man from Fort Lauderdale. He was built like an offensive lineman of a pro football team and often carried himself as such, having played most of his life despite not making the cut at several pro tryouts. Tone was usually well dressed and wore expensive jewelry and shoes.

"I appreciate it bro. Trying to make it happen out here," Tone lit the cigar in his hand. "Darcy wanted to be some hoes and not bring me on staff, it's all good though."

Derek was the only one who did not have a cigar in his hand or a glass of alcohol in front of him.

"These cigars are overhyped," Preston said, looking at the cigar in his hand, disappointed.

Preston, born and raised in Richmond, Virginia, was fresh out of law school. He was often given a hard time from the group because of his 'good hair' and bright eye color, which caused people to classify him as a 'pretty boy'. Preston and Derek were the only two in the group that were in relationships.

"Yeah, these are trash. Why did y'all want to meet at this spot again?" Elle asked.

"Preston wanted to come up here—you know he try to be upper echelon," Tone said.

"I was cool with getting some wings, a brew, and calling it a day," Preston told them as they waved him off.

“I feel like we can’t even talk in here, this like a library bro,” Elle shook his head and sat his cigar down.

Elle, born and raised in Los Angeles, was an industrial compliance engineer. He was tall and skinny, body covered in quite a few tattoos, some of which were covered by his short sleeve collared shirt. Elliot’s exposure to street violence most of his life contributed to his short fuse back in his college days. It was not something he glorified or bragged about as did many who wanted people to view them as tough. Elliot calmed down tremendously since his younger days.

“Tone is doing things, Preston about to be a lawyer, Derek, you still holding it down, always good to see the team striving bro. It’s better than what they give us credit for, you know?” Elle said.

“We been talking about the day we could stack up since college, putting dollars together to buy a full chicken box,” Preston said. “We almost at the top of the food chain fellas. Keep grinding.”

Preston finished the rest of his drink and slammed the glass down, which was the loudest action that happened in the smoke room.

“Stack up and rack up…these hoes,” Tone laughed as he shook hands with Preston, who agreed with him.

"P, you still with Tiara?" Derek asked, his voice tinged with a scolding sarcasm.

Preston and Tone stopped and looked at each other, then laughed to one another.

"The feds right here," Preston made them all laugh again. "Yeah D, we are good, she's good. I'm sure she would appreciate you asking."

"Hey," Derek held his hands up in innocence. "You know she always watching you."

"Nah, she won't find anything on me, nothing to see. I'm on the righteous path." Preston smiled as the others frowned.

"Since when?" Tone asked sarcastically.

"He can't help but lie," Elle said. "He lies for a living."

"Y'all act like I'm just out here bad." Preston's sinister grin made it evident that he was usually up to no good.

"Just accept that you a hoe bro," Elle chuckled. "And we not judging you, we are all for doing your thing. Lord knows we all do, but don't play the role bro."

"Derek is the pure one," Tone said.

"Yeah, *now* he is." Preston looked over at Derek. "He had his days of filth."

“Those days are over,” Derek said and grabbed his glass of water.

“Yeah whatever, those days not that long ago,” Preston said with his eyebrows raised, causing them all to agree. “Derek was running through the church rats and got converted.”

“Not the church rats!” Tone threw his hands up.

“I swear I feel like I’m gon’ get struck down one day standing next to P I swear,” Elle made them all laugh again.

“You not right, bro,” Derek shook his head with a smirk on his face.

“What’s up with you and Katie though?” Preston asked.

“Everything is cool. We heading to this lake trip with her family this weekend,” he said, causing them to start exaggerating about the trip.

“Going on the family trip, he about to come back engaged,” Tone said.

Laughter erupted, but quickly died down as Derek sat there quiet with a straight face. They all suddenly moved in closer to him.

“Something you want to tell us?” Preston leaned in with an intense look on his face.

"You know you can't stay in the game forever," Derek said.

"Bruh why not?" Tone asked.

"Man shut up," Elle said, playfully hitting Tone in the arm.

"We been together long enough; it's time to go ahead and lock it down," Derek said.

He was now in the middle with the three of them standing around his bar stool. Although he was sure of his decision, the way they looked at him and asked him questions made him feel an uneasy pressure. He anticipated that it would be that way when he broke the news to them.

"And you are sure she is it?" Preston asked.

"Come on man. Y'all know I was sure about her since we got to Darcy," Derek said.

Each of them witnessed the highs and lows of Derek's pursuit of Katie all throughout college and the short period after college. They were fully aware of the history.

"But is she pressuring you?" Preston continued with the questions. "Like is this what you really want to do?"

One would easily be able to see how Preston was an attorney. He asked many questions, dissected everything that a person said, and was very good at planting seeds of doubt. It was something that made him difficult to be lied to but made him too good of a liar himself.

"This is what I want to do. I don't want nobody else, so why not?" Derek responded.

"I think it's cool as long as she not still playing games. You know I don't trust women at all," Elle said. "They are worse than we are."

"Exactly, we have too much to lose just to be putting a ring on somebody. And with this generation of women?" Preston shook his head as he grabbed his glass that the bar tender refilled.

"That was a long time ago, we were in college. Everybody was young back then, we are grown now, everything has been cool— "

"I'm not talking about college; I'm talking about what she was on when you first started talking to her heavy. When we almost had to see about homie she was messing with," Elle said with slight elevation his voice.

"I'm not even on that," Preston stood right in front of Derek. "I want to know why *you* want to do it. I get why she wants to do it; women want all that— the wedding, the ring, flex for these other hoes, I get all that. But I don't get why *you* want to do this. I know you love her, I'm not questioning that, that's what's up. But if y'all got a good thing, what's the rush for real?"

Not one smile appeared on Preston's face as he continued to interrogate.

"Why you keep questioning the man?" Tone asked.

"Nah man, this our brother and I'm just trying to make sure he good," Preston said to them all. "None of these women out here can be trusted, none of them. Not one. Not any of the ones you know," he pointed to Elle. "None of the ones you know." He then pointed at Tone. "Not mine, and not yours," he said to Derek, who found himself begin to get irritated. "You might not wanna' hear it, and Katie is cool, but she is still a woman. She is still one of these women of our generation."

Elle and Tone nodded in agreement with Preston. Derek sat staring at him, trying to maintain his composure as Preston continued to speak.

"We don't get anything out of marrying them, it's all for them. They get it all, what part of it benefits us? It's like a war out here, and a lot of these women trying to play like men, trying to get a lick off us first. I see it too many times."

"You really about to discourage the man from marrying his girl?" Tone asked.

“I’m not saying that. I am not saying that,” Preston defended himself as the two of them began to go back and forth. “I’m just saying make sure that’s who you want to do this with.”

The conversation between the four of them started to become intense. Preston continued to elaborate more as Elle and Tone added to it. While they did not disagree with some of what Preston said, the two of them did not want him to discourage Derek. The entire conversation frustrated Derek overall, he felt like the conversation was an attack on Katie personally even though they spoke about women in general.

“D, whatever you do, we support you. We are brothers so you know we got you either way,” Tone told him.

“Exactly, I’m not trying to come at you or her, I’m just giving you the real. I’m about to chill now though because I’m killing the vibe,” Preston took another drink and turned towards the bar.

The rest of them agreed, going back to their usual pace of conversation as if the exchange didn’t happen. Although the conversation went back to normal and they shook hands with Derek, he still felt the uncomfortable tension from the conversation. Despite laughing from the jokes and going along to get along, the conflict was still there in his mind.

Some of his closest friends questioned the connection that he had with the woman he planned on settling down with; a conflict that he felt would shake anyone. On the drive home, he didn't turn on the radio. He replayed the conversation repeatedly in his mind, which led to him thinking back to the beginning and when seeds of doubt were first planted…

CHAPTER 12

Charlotte, NORTH CAROLINA

Two Years Ago.

Moving was always tedious, and it was something that Katie hoped she wouldn't have to do again for quite a while. She pushed the front door of her apartment open, revealing a new and empty space apart from her couch and a few boxes that were stacked against the wall. When she pushed the heavy black door open, she wandered in and collapsed onto the couch, immediately closing her eyes. Her grey sweats were covered in dust, marks, and a few snags of hanging thread. Derek shortly followed behind, pushing a stack of boxes in on a dolly. He pushed them against the wall, and then leaned against the stack of boxes to rest. She and Derek spent most of the day moving the remainder of her things out of storage and into her apartment. Katie was glad to be back in Charlotte having just moved back from New York a week prior, but she hated the whole process of unpacking and setting up her apartment. She stayed with Derek until the apartment was ready.

"This is a nice spot, so clean and new," Derek said.

"They just built this complex," Katie said to him. "It's a whole new place."

Katie began to sit up slowly to get back up and help. Before she could stand up, Derek held his hand up signaling for her to sit back down.

"Relax, I got it," Derek said.

Katie, without dispute, quickly lay back down on the couch in relief. She then kicked off her tennis shoes, causing Derek to make a face of disgust. She was not wearing any socks.

"No socks on though?" Derek shook his head and pinched his nostrils together.

"Shut up," Katie said, voice muffled due to her lying face down on the couch.

Derek stood and stared at Katie for a moment. Even when she was dressed down, she was so beautiful to him. This was a moment that he thought about for years and still could not believe that he was with the woman that he always wanted. It was the reason that all the moving and hours he spent on a Saturday did not feel like work at all. The two of them began to date exclusively four months prior, which played a factor in Katie making the choice to move back to Charlotte.

The random silence made Katie open her eyes, catching Derek staring at her, causing him to quickly begin moving boxes and unpack them. Katie grinned before hastily getting up to walk to the bathroom. As soon as she went in the bathroom, she began coughing; coughing then became throwing up. Katie didn't feel well most of the day. Derek planned to cater to her and take care of her. He was anxious to prove that he would be a good man to her, to show her how he always wanted to sweep her off her feet.

The sound of Katie's phone vibrating on the kitchen island interrupted his thoughts. The vibration of the phone on the marble countertop caused it to slide across the island and eventually hit the floor. Derek walked over to pick it up quickly; having a sense of urgency since the phone was new and did not have a case to protect it. The phone did not have a password configured to it yet, so the phone was unlocked when Derek picked it up. The numerous message notifications on the screen immediately caught Derek's attention. Some were from a group thread between her and some of her friends, but the others were all were from one name: Isaac. When Derek saw Isaac's name, he felt his heart rate speed up and his face began to feel hot as he opened the message thread.

"Are you okay out there?" Katie asked loudly from behind the bathroom door.

The question was ironic seeing as to how Katie was the one throwing up in the bathroom. Derek didn't respond; he was too glued to what he was reading on Katie's phone. The first message that he saw included a picture of a gold Rolex: *'Had to bring this out today, made me think of you'* As Derek scrolled up, there were five more pictures. Four of them were of Katie sitting at a restaurant table with a smirk on her face. It was evident that Isaac was the one that took the pictures and was sitting right across from her. The final picture was of her and Isaac making silly faces at the camera. He was standing behind her, his arm extended in front of them so that he could take the picture. The two of them looked comfortable with each other, a little too comfortable for Derek. Isaac had a low haircut, but it was evident that his hair was thinning and that he was becoming bald. He also had a five-o-clock shadow on his face, showing that there was potential for a beard to grow there. The feeling of Katie's cold hand on his shoulder snapped him out of his daze; her hand was cold due to the cold water from the bathroom faucet. Derek didn't even hear her come out of the bathroom.

"Are you okay?" Katie asked softly.

Derek turned around to see a concerned look on Katie's face, which turned into confusion when she noticed that Derek was angry. She noticed her phone in his hand but didn't make one mention of it. His facial expression never allowed him to hide how he truly felt, it always revealed what was going on in his mind.

"What's wrong?" Katie then asked.

Derek held the phone up so that Katie could see the pictures that he looked through. Her facial expression changed slightly, but she was not concerned or startled.

"You really went through my phone?"

"That's all you have to say?" Derek's voice began to elevate. "This is what you were on when I wasn't around?"

"Why are you getting loud?" Katie glanced at the wall then looked back at Derek. "These walls are paper thin, so lower— "

"Answer my question," Derek snapped. "What is this about?"

"Those are old, before me and you were anything."

"Old? These were from a few months ago! This was in like December. You think I'm stupid?"

Derek forcefully threw the phone at the couch, causing Katie to flinch. When Derek threw the phone, Katie then became angry.

"Nobody is calling you stupid! I just told you those pictures are old, so what are you so mad about?"

"You still texting and talking to him! That is what I'm mad about. You just can't let him go; he just has to be in your life huh?"

Derek's aggressive pacing around the room caused Katie to become even more angry.

"Okay! How long have you been holding that in?" Katie stepped closer to Derek. "You are going off and throwing a tantrum about some pictures, even though I keep telling you they're old! There is no way I can control what someone sends to me. You think I'm lying?"

"I don't know what to think to be real with you; he seemed real comfortable texting you and sending you pictures, and he seems to be happy with the expensive watch that you bought him too. But you act like you can't control it, you act like you can't block the number, man miss me with that," Derek waved her off.

Isaac Duke, Katie's ex-boyfriend, was a name that got underneath Derek's skin and a face that he hated to see. Isaac also graduated from Darcy; he was a year ahead of Katie and Derek. He was a very well-known finance major like Katie, which put them in many of the same courses. Derek and his friends were not too fond of Isaac or his crew. It did not make it any better that Isaac had the girl Derek always wanted wrapped around his finger at one point.

"Derek…" Katie started.

Derek sat at the kitchen island, staring off into space with an angry scowl.

"Did Isaac visit me while I lived in New York? Yes, he did. Was he in New York for me? No!" she said emphatically. "His whole family is in Brooklyn. Nothing happened. Nothing is going to happen. I bought that watch years ago. It is the last thing that you need to be worried about, the last thing. I'm here with you, not with him. If I wanted to be with him, I would be."

Derek turned in his chair and looked at her; still angry but finally able to lower his voice.

"Why you even go hang with him though? If we already started talking, you didn't even need to go meet up with him, that's what I'm saying."

Katie shook her head and let out a sigh.

"I don't know what all that is for. You got this started," Derek continued.

"At that time, yeah, we started to talk consistently, but I was not in a relationship with you. If I wanted to go somewhere, hang with somebody, I could do that. Talking to someone and being in a relationship with someone are not the same thing, what we were then is not what we are now."

When Katie said that, Derek looked at her in disappointment. He then got up and walked towards the front door.

"Really? You just walk off while I'm talking to you?" Katie asked, a small tremble in her voice.

Derek stopped and then slowly turned around to face her.

"You have always been one to play games. That's always been the type of chick you are. For years, I dealt with you playing, putting up with the wrong dudes, and even now after all that time and I think you are finally giving something good a chance, you still playing. I'm done wasting my time."

Derek, hurt and disappointed, walked out and slammed the door behind him. He began to feel as if his dream come true was a nightmare…

CHAPTER 13

Charlotte, NORTH CAROLINA

6AM – Present Day

The airport was empty at six in the morning. The check-in lines and TSA lines were not long, so people made it to their gates quickly with no disruption. Derek sat at his flight's gate; head rested against the window with his ears snugged by his headphones. Traveling was the one aspect of Derek's job that he enjoyed. His manager Chuck told him short notice that he needed to do a new client on-boarding since he had time-off coming up at the end of the week. Chuck gave Derek a huge break by sending him to his hometown of Chicago as opposed to Denver, which was initially where Derek was scheduled to go.

"I really don't understand what you get out of being up this early every day," Derek grumbled to Katie over the phone, rubbing his eyes. "I am exhausted, I keep yawning."

While Derek sounded terrible, Katie sounded as if she'd been up for hours. It was not difficult for her to wake up early and get going. Although Derek knew the night before that he would have to be up early in the morning, it wasn't enough to motivate him to go to bed early.

"So, you are going home…" Katie said. "That's cool that you get to spend time with momma Gloria!"

Derek chuckled, "Momma Gloria huh?"

"She loves me, and I love her," Katie said. "Which is a major thing if you didn't know."

"Is it?" Derek looked out the window as his plane finally pulled up to the gate.

"I hope you are joking, absolutely it is! Some women's lives are hell because they gotta' compete with an overbearing momma, so I'm thankful. Some women are in love with their sons."

"Sounds like you know from experience," Derek said as passengers began to rush off the plane and flood the gate area.

"Unfortunately," she said. "Thank the Lord I left that where it was."

"Wow, that bad?"

"It can be overbearing but I understand it. I take people's parents seriously, and my mom's relationship with my future husband. What my mom thinks means a lot to me."

Derek, some years back, didn't think much of parental blessing at all. Initially, what a person's parents thought about him was meaningless to him. He always felt that it was antiquated to interact with someone's parents. However, his mindset evolved the more he hung around older seasoned men and developed a new understanding of respect.

"What about your dad though?" Derek said. "Your mom is cool. I don't know much about your pops, and he probably don't know much about me. He probably doesn't even know you with me."

"You can't be serious. Stop it. After all this time? He knows about you," Katie said.

"Yeah, but I don't know him, nothing about him."

"I know, but that will change this weekend since we are seeing everyone. I just want the one that is special to me to blend in with the most special people to me."

Katie's comment made Derek feel good, it gave him a refreshing reminder that their relationship was going in the right direction and growing deeper roots.

"This is Tasha calling me, text me when you land, love you, bye," she clicked over before Derek could say anything.

He simply sighed and leaned his head back against the window, still waking up.

“I hope I can blend.”

CHAPTER 14

Chicago, ILLINOIS

"How in the world is it only thirty degrees in April? Good grief!" The cackling laugh that followed the statement was nails on a chalkboard to Derek's ears.

The technical engineer that he was with, Ben, was the one to whom the laugh belonged. He drove to Chicago a day prior from Cincinnati where he had to complete an on-boarding audit for another new client. Ben was the one that handled the deep and technical analytics of the devices on premise and their performance, which required quite a few certifications to be able to do. He addressed all the technical questions while Derek walked through the basics. Ben's job was where the real money was. He was a tall Caucasian man in his late thirties who already had much grey in his hair. It did not take long for one to figure out that Ben was a very sarcastic person, and often came off as rude to those that couldn't handle his humor.

The flurries from the previous week left small mounds of snow scattered across the city, few of which persisted under the sunlight. Derek and Ben met at the client site. After Derek gave his usual spiel and answered questions, he allowed Ben to do the rest of the talking from there. His boss Chuck always told him that he needed to be more engaging with new clients, but Derek struggled to do so due to his lack of interest. He was anxious to get the onboard session over with so that he could begin to make his rounds to see his family and some old friends if he had time. The client was an IT Director in his fifties, he and Ben were talking about baseball and other common interests. Derek quickly became the odd man out as those two talked and laughed. After an hour and a half, the audit was complete.

"You need a ride to your hotel? Where are you staying?" Ben asked as they walked out.

"Nah, I'm good. This is home," Derek said as he put his messenger bag strap over his shoulder, huge grin on his face. "I'll do the write up of all that we went over and email it to you later."

Derek was anxious to get to his mother's house. His mind hadn't been on work since he landed in Chicago. As he sat on the train, the smile he had initially turned into a straight face and eventually a scowl. He quickly remembered that he wasn't in Charlotte any longer. The ride on the train gave him memories of his younger days; he knew the city like the back of his hand. The train was able to get him within walking distance of his mother's house. As the train began to slow down, a huge billboard came into view: YOUR BROTHER'S LIFE MATTERS. Below it in smaller letters it read: *Stop the Violence.* Several of the friends that he grew up with were either in prison, recently released from prison, or dead. Despite all of it, Derek hated how people outside of Chicago painted Chicago with a broad brush. He hated the nicknames, the comments, and how the entire city was known for the actions of a few. For him, it was home, and the place that made him into who he was.

When he stepped off the train and began to walk, even more memories flooded his mind. He hadn't been home since the previous summer. The houses in his old neighborhood were much older houses with small yards. Some of the people that lived there when Derek was a child were still around. A few young men—ranging from early teens to early twenties—stood not too far from a storefront talking to one another and pointing up the street. As Derek walked on the opposite side of the street, he realized that he recognized a few of them. They were small kids the last time he saw them, he was taken aback by how much they'd grown. He quickened his step when his mother's house came into view. When Derek rang the doorbell, an older woman appeared in the door shortly thereafter. She was a shorter petite woman in her sixties, a head full of grey hair, and a large smile.

"There he is!" she shouted as she swung open the screen door.

Derek gave her a long hug as soon as he stepped into the doorway. His grandmother Mary, whom everyone called Mattie, gave the best hugs.

"I'm cooking so there will be food for you to eat tonight," Mattie said as she walked back towards the kitchen. "Your mom told me you are here until the morning."

There was not a uniformed theme in the house apart from all the walls being white. Family pictures were hung along the walls, showing glimpses of childhood and adulthood. A huge picture of Derek on stage during his high school graduation covered the wall above the television stand.

"Your mom is up at the school; she is supposed to be leaving around four," Mattie said as she washed a pot out in the kitchen sink.

"Yeah, I'm actually about to go surprise her. She's about to eat in about half-hour." Derek walked into the kitchen.

"How you know? You spoke to her today?" Mattie sat down at the kitchen table and pulled a cigarette out of the carton on the table.

“Grandma you know she has had the same routine for years. I probably need to get to the train to make it in time.”

When Derek mentioned the train, Mattie looked at him and frowned. She then rolled her eyes as Derek looked off into space, waiting.

“Boy, you are not slick, my keys are on the living room table,” Mattie said, causing Derek to quickly hug her and give her a kiss on the cheek.

“Go on now,” she pushed him off with a grin on her face.

Derek rushed out of the house, glad to have access to a car. Mattie’s small green car was parked up on the curb in front of the house. The smell of cigarettes hit his nostrils as soon as he got in the car, Mattie’s beat up black leather bible rested on the passenger seat. Before Derek put the keys in the ignition, he watched as two of the young boys he saw by the storefront earlier came into view up the street. They were running full speed down the street, and then cut between two houses out of sight. A police car quickly turned down the street and sped past Derek, then began to slow down slowly driving past each house. Derek more than ever felt that he was back at home, an environment that was outside of the bubble that he grew accustomed to back in Charlotte.

The city that made you…

CHAPTER 15

Charlotte, NORTH CAROLINA

Grace Gospel Center

"Oh my God."

Katie sat in Tasha's office, savaging through her lunch as if she hadn't eaten in days. She suddenly stopped when she glanced up to see Tasha staring at her, eyebrows raised.

"Chile' is there something I need to know? Are you in need?"

"Am I that bad?" Katie grabbed a napkin.

"Girl, yes." Tasha tossed Katie an additional paper towel.

Tasha Marshall, a rather tall, motherly woman from Mobile, Alabama, was one of the directors at GGC. She was over all community outreach, volunteer initiatives, and hospitality. Katie decided to meet with Tasha during her lunch break since her lunch breaks were an hour long. No one would notice that she was not at her desk even if she chose to take longer. Any opportunity she could take to get away from the office, she would take it. Katie always kept to herself at work, whether the office was quiet or festive. She was one of very few women in her office and one of five black employees in her office. There was not much that she could talk to her coworkers about or any common ground where she felt she could connect with them, so she stayed at her desk to herself. She developed a reputation of being anti-social, and that was exactly how she wanted it to be.

"I know you don't have that much time, and I definitely don't need you doing ninety to get back to work."

Tasha leaned on her desk beside Katie, looking at the food she was eating.

"What is with all the shots at me today?"

"Girl you know you drive like a bat out of hell, it is not a secret," Tasha made Katie laugh. "I pray for additional traveling mercy every time I ride with you. And that music…I heard it when you were all the way up the street!"

Katie rolled her eyes as she looked back down at her food.

"So… starting next week, I am going to be stepping down temporarily from outreach, and hospitality," Tasha said.

Katie's eyes widened as she licked her fingertips.

"What? Why?"

"You have probably noticed by now that Jeff has not been here the last few weeks, right?" Tasha asked.

Jeff was Tasha's husband of twenty-three years. He was also one of the elders.

"I'm telling you because I know you won't go around gossiping about it. He has been going through some serious depression. I mean questioning his faith, questioning if he wants to stay married, everything. He just has not been in a good place, so I need to be there with him. You will still see me on some Sundays, but as for everything else…" Tasha threw up the peace sign.

"Wow, I will definitely pray for him. He is such a good man," Katie said. "For you too. You are a strong woman to endure that."

"Yes, please keep the both of us in prayer," Tasha said.

"You don't want to keep busy to keep your mind off of it?" Katie asked.

"Katie," Tasha shook her head. "He is my husband, my priority before anything else—including GGC."

"Wow," Katie's eyes widened. "Don't let them hear you say that."

"Listen…" Tasha scooted in closer. "Your home has to be your priority. Nothing should take precedent over your family. What good is any of this without family?"

"That is true," Katie closed her container of food. "You just don't hear people value family like that anymore."

"Because people are all about self," Tasha walked over to one of the bookshelves in her office. "It's not even just in church, it is career wise, everything. If you are not willing to sacrifice, don't get married. But I'm done preaching to you!"

"No sister! Bring us on home!" Katie yelled dramatically as they both laughed. "So, who is taking over for you while you are out?"

Tasha turned around and a huge smile spread across her face, making her cheeks bigger than they already were. Katie's eyes widened and she began to shake her head.

"Oh no you didn't…" Katie said with a frown. "Tasha!"

"Why not you?" Tasha walked over and playfully hugged Katie while she sat in her chair.

"I am nobody's director. I can't run three committees; I just don't have the patience for it,"

Katie's voice was muffled by Tasha's arm slightly covering her mouth during the hug.

"You will be fine! It is not all going to fall on you; I will make sure you have help, and you know you will be working under Elder Daniels anyway. You know who Elder Daniels is right?"

"Oh, I know who he is," Katie said strongly. "Trust me."

"I'm not even going to entertain that," Tasha said. "But to be real with you, nobody else but you came to mind when they asked me. Trust me, I will make sure you have all that you need."

Katie sat still frowning at Tasha, but deep down knew that she was going to give in. The biggest pull was that Tasha was the one asking, and it was very hard for Katie to ever say no to her. As her facial expression began to show surrender, Tasha's smile reappeared.

"I'll do it."

Tasha began to clap and cheer in excitement.

"Perfect, perfect! I will let them know."

She got on her computer and began typing up an email, using her long sky-blue nails instead of her actual fingers. Katie began to pack her leftovers to get ready to head back to work.

"You're out of town this weekend, right?" Tasha asked, still typing.

"Yep, lake house trip with the family. I'm leaving Friday," Katie said.

"How are you and your dad?" Tasha asked.

Katie felt a sudden sense of anxiety. The question caused her to become tense. Tasha immediately noticed the change in Katie's demeanor and body language.

"We're good. No problems there."

Tasha stopped typing and looked up at Katie.

"You know what I mean. Have you two been communicating?" Tasha' pulled her glasses off, eyes locked on Katie.

Katie looked for the words to say as she glanced at Tasha bashfully.

"You two have not spoken, have you?" Tasha asked strongly. "You never reached out like I told you, did you?"

"Tasha, I don't need to. We don't have a problem with each other, so we're good," Katie said, slightly irritated.

"No, no ma'am. I told you, the things we have talked about in here and what we have agreed about, you need to tell him. Your dad is a major part of you, especially now that you are bringing someone else into the equation. You have not spoken to him in almost three years. That is not okay."

Tasha knew this conversation was one that Katie hated to have, but she did not care. It took a while for her to get Katie to be transparent with her, but when it finally happened, it was a lot more than she anticipated. Katie was open to Tasha much about her family dynamic and her relationship with her father, things that she hadn't spoken with anyone about.

"I get it, we're going on this lake house trip. I will be able to talk then."

"You are bringing another man to your family trip, to interact with your father who you have not spoken with in almost three years. The two of you are not on good terms; does Derek even know what he is getting himself into? I know you have not told him everything because it took you forever to tell me."

Katie gathered her things and prepared to leave. "Just let me know what you need for me to do when it's time."

Tasha stared Katie down as she walked out of the office. Katie got into her Jeep and sat for a moment to gather her thoughts.

He could not care less if I did have something to say to him.

CHAPTER 16

Chicago, ILLINOIS

Same DAY.

The level of joy that Gloria Pierce felt was evident by how much she smiled at her son across the table from her, who blushed at all the compliments that she gave him. Derek drove up to Gloria's job to take her to lunch, a surprise to her. She was one of the counselors at a middle school in the inner city. The two of them went to a Mexican restaurant that was not far from Gloria's school, a restaurant that they used to frequent back when Derek lived in Chicago.

"You just get more and more handsome every time I see you," Gloria's smile beamed with pride.

Gloria, like her mother Mary, was a woman of small stature. She was short and did not have much weight on her, Derek easily towered over her. Gloria's soft voice and gentle spirit often gave people the impression that she could be pushed over and easily taken advantage of. The wire-framed glasses that rested on her face added to that perception, but people learned quickly that it was the furthest from the truth. Gloria meant the world to Derek, and he meant the world to her. Witnessing how much she sacrificed to take care of him growing up made him willing to do anything for her at any time. Derek was not Gloria's first child, but she suffered a miscarriage at the age of seventeen.

"Too bad you're only here until the morning; we could have gone to your cousin's game this weekend," she said.

"I know. Uncle Don told me he's nice now. I saw a few clips on him online," Derek said as he cut into the remainder of the burrito on his plate.

"Yep, and Justin has gotten so tall," Gloria shook her head at the thought of it. "I told Don I know that height came from our side because Jeanie's side is all short."

Derek nodded as he worked on chewing all of the food in his mouth.

"I need to come and visit you; I'm long overdue."

Gloria made Derek frown in skepticism.

"Don't even start," Gloria said, trying to hold back her laugh.

"Come down in June," he said. "The weather will be nice, a lot to do, proposing, fun stuff."

Gloria froze and her mouth dropped. She quickly grabbed Derek's cup out of his hand when he tried to take another sip, making him burst into laughter.

"Excuse me? Come again?" Her eyes were wide in excitement. "Stop playing around."

"I'm not playing, I'm serious," Derek said.

"That is perfect! I hope she knows that she is getting one of the good ones, oh my God, I'm just so…" she held hand over her heart.

Derek began to blush again.

"But you have a good one too, I hope you know that. It's hard these days, I see a lot of these women and Lord…hold on to that one, she is what you need."

Gloria was very fond of Katie, having met her for the first time when she came to Chicago with Derek during the summer of their first year together. The two of them immediately connected when they found common interest in certain television shows and their love for sports. Gloria was always a fan of basketball; she became even more of a fan when Derek began to play. Katie was into sports only because her father was into sports. As a child, she loved the time the two of them spent together when he took her to games or when they watched together at home. Apart from sports and television shows, Gloria loved how Katie treated Derek and how she carried herself as a young woman. Katie showed herself to be trustworthy, and that was very important to Gloria.

"I'm telling her parents this weekend," Derek said.

Gloria noticed the change of tone in his voice. She then put her hand on top of his.

"That didn't sound too assuring. What's that about?"

The two of them got up to leave when Derek's phone alarm went off. The restaurant was empty; they were two of five people in the entire place.

"I just don't know if I will connect with her people like that, mainly her dad. I haven't even spoke to him. What if they think I'm no good or I'm not up to what they think she should have? It would've been nice to have a solid relationship with them before trying to talk to them about something like this," Derek said.

Gloria nodded, not responding as they walked outside. When Derek went to open the passenger door for her, she stopped and stared at him.

"What have I always told you since you were little?"

A slight grin came across his face as he was face to face with his mother.

"Come on, tell me."

“I’m either going to make my way or get in my own way. No one can stop me like I can,” he said.

“That’s right. If you go and interact with them or anybody…thinking you have to try to measure up or that you need to be more than who you are, you will end up in over your head,” she put her hand on his cheek. “You are a good man, honorable, and respectful. But if you devalue yourself, you give people no reason to value you. Even if someone does not like you, they can’t deny that about you.”

Derek smiled and gave her a tight hug. Gloria never allowed anyone to be down on themselves or speak negatively about themselves. It was something that she was very serious about, especially working with students. Derek drove her back up to the school, the two of them had at least eight minutes to spare before her lunch break was over.

“Don’t get food tonight; we’re cooking,” Gloria said as she got out of the car. “Are you going to see your dad?”

Derek nodded. Gloria looked away again for a moment, searching for her next words.

“Well, your dad doesn’t stay with your grandma anymore,” Gloria said, causing Derek’s eyes to widen. “He’s at Valerie’s house; you know how I’ve always felt about you on that side of town. But call her.”

Valerie was Derek's aunt; he had no idea that his father stayed there. Derek did not bother to call because he knew his aunt's neighborhood all too well. It was a place where much of Derek's troubles from his youth dwelled and awaited him, a place that Derek almost didn't make it out of.

CHAPTER 17

Chicago, ILLINOIS

Derek spent much time in his aunt's neighborhood in his younger years. As he drove through, memories of the calm, tranquil place contrasted jarringly with the now festive and bustling streets. Gloria put an end to the time that Derek spent around there when he was fifteen. She believed that if Derek continued to spend time with the people that he hung around; he would have ended up in a bad place. Getting over the loss of her first child was difficult for Gloria when she was younger, so she refused to allow anything to put Derek at risk. Derek pulled onto his aunt's block and parked up the street, there was not much open space in front of her house.

"The honorable minister Dupree!" someone yelled.

The sound of a front door closing quickly followed. Derek turned to see a man standing on the porch of the house across the street, holding his arms up with a large smile on his face. Derek immediately recognized who it was, and a huge smile came across his face as well. He jogged across the street and the two of them greeted each other with a loud laugh, handshake, and a hug.

"You disappeared! Where you been?" Derek asked.

"I can say the same about you, right? I been laying low. What's good though? You grew up!"

The man looked Derek up and down, as if in a proud disbelief that Derek was the same person he once knew. Roman Douglas, known to everyone as Rome, was one of the people that Derek spent much time with when he was younger. Rome, along with his best friend Jerrod, were well known in the city. Rome was the reason many knew who Derek was, he and Jerrod took Derek under their wing. The two of them met Derek during a pick-up game at the park, some boys wanted to fight Derek after they lost a bet because Derek won. Rome, who was fourteen at the time, stepped in to defend him, lifting his shirt to show a gun on his waistband. It was the first time Derek, who was eleven, saw a gun in real life. It was with Jerrod and Rome that Derek first shot a gun when he turned thirteen. Rome was also the one that facilitated Derek losing his virginity at the age of fourteen. A girl that lived in the neighborhood, known to be promiscuous, was the one that Rome had convinced to do it. She too was three years older than Derek was.

“Don’t ever fall in love with it,” Rome would tell him. “It’s you today, somebody else tomorrow—could be me. Just get yours and keep it pushing. They are never really *yours*; it’s just your turn.”

The experience was Derek’s first exposure to sex, and everything about women that he learned came from the older boys that he was around during his young years. His view on commitment and remaining detached grew from the conversations and experiences he’d had with them. If Derek was honest with himself, that mindset governed many of his high school and college relationships. He enjoyed relationships for the time that he was in them, but at the first sign of trouble, he would end them using his mindset to justify it. As he learned more, grew closer to God, and began pursuing Katie, his new mindset constantly warred against the old one.

Derek lost contact with a lot of the people he used to run with after Jerrod was killed one night in a shootout with some others from a different neighborhood, one of the scariest nights of Derek’s life. It was a night that he felt he was going to lose his life, and one of the last nights that he saw Rome.

“I heard you a preacher now; left the hood and became a pulpit pimp.”

Rome leaned against the car that was beside him. His dark eyes and his slightly weathered face made him look a little older than he actually was.

"Nah, where you hear that?"

"People talk. They show me some of the posts you put up. You sound like one to me," Rome pulled the cigarette from behind his ear, which was hidden by his thick black hair. "I respect it."

Rome's chuckling quickly turned into coughing. The coughing did not stop him from relighting his cigarette and taking a few drags. He then looked up the street and nodded towards Derek's aunt's house.

"Going to see Val?"

"Yeah, pops staying there now. I'm about to go see him," Derek said.

"I didn't know the OG was in there," he flicked the cigarette to the ground. "I'm not gon' hold you though," Rome shook Derek's hand and hugged him. "Good to see you show your face back in the hood. If you still around tonight hit me, a lot of the gang ain' seen you in a long time."

Rome headed to the train to get to work. He was one of the last people that Derek expected to see when he came back to Chicago. Derek also knew for a fact that nothing good would come out of him hanging with some old faces from the neighborhood.

As Derek made his way towards his Aunt Valerie's house, a cat came into view resting on a pallet right near the front door. The front door was slightly open and opened a little wider as the cat ran back inside. Derek then heard a voice speaking to the cat not long after it ran back inside. A rather tall woman, lighter skinned, with short hair came into view cleaning up the living room when he walked in. What stood out about her the most was that her upper body was much smaller than her lower body.

"There he is!" she yelled in excitement when she saw Derek. "I haven't seen you in so long!"

She gave him a long hug. The two of them sat and caught up on life—primarily Derek's life. They hadn't spent much time together since Derek was young. Valerie enjoyed seeing him and spending time with him.

"I'm so proud of you, grown into such a good man," she said.

"I'm trying," Derek said modestly.

"Trying? You're doing it!" Valerie smiled. "You are doing it king."

"How long pops been staying here?" Derek asked.

"It's been about two months now, he's up there, staying in the guest room."

"How that happen?" Derek asked her.

Valerie sighed and sat her glass of lemonade on the table.

"So, you know he was at the VA for a little while, that woman he was staying with put him out. Her house got broken into and it had something to do with…you know," she motioned her hand. "He bounced around; didn't have anywhere to go. But he started using a little bit instead of just selling, which is why they didn't let him stay at the VA. Of course, he had run ins with the police, and they were just about to put him in jail. You know when they don't know what to do with folks, they just try to throw them in jail," she rolled her eyes. "I was hesitant about letting him come here. I told him if he wanted to stay here, he was going to have to work and leave all that alone."

The unspoken truth was Derek's father's involvement with drugs, something he started in his early adult years. He used to be a well-known high school athlete in Illinois, known for football, basketball, and track. A drastic knee injury derailed his plans to play college football. It was a time of embarrassment and humility for him. He did not want to become just another failure stuck in the city that did not do much with his life. On impulse, he enlisted himself in the army. The decision frustrated Derek's mother Gloria because Derek was a baby and she felt that his father, Maurice, was only worried about himself. She viewed it as him fleeing from being a father, causing a strong hatred to stir up in her heart. Maurice spent a few years in the army, he wrote occasionally and called occasionally. When he returned, he got more involved in Derek's young life and finally exposed Derek more to his father's side of the family, including Valerie. Maurice spent several years involved in the streets while Derek was left to be raised by the streets.

Derek made his way up the stairs of the house. The sound of snoring interrupted the silence as he came closer to one of the rooms. The door was wide open, the TV was on the sports channel, but the volume was so low that it might as well had been muted. Derek's father Maurice was asleep on the bed, mouth open, an open bag of chips rested on top of his stomach accompanied by crumbs scattered around. Maurice was a tall man with very large hands; he still had a muscular build although his stomach hung over his waistline. He still had a head full of hair, just with much more grey hair mixed in now that he was older. Most of Derek's physical attributes came from his father. Maurice woke himself up with his snoring, causing Derek to laugh.

"Look at him," Maurice sat up and put his feet to the floor, then reached out and shook Derek's hand. "What are you doing here?"

"I'm in town for my job, just wanted to see y'all while I'm here."

Derek sat in a computer chair that was in the room. Maurice was happy and surprised to see his son. The two of them had the same mannerisms, same laugh; no one could deny that they were father and son. But after a few minutes of small talk, the dialogue ran dry.

"So, what else?" Maurice asked abruptly.

Derek shrugged. "Just been working and that's about it really."

"Your mom told you I'm staying here?"

Derek nodded. Maurice simply nodded back. He was always one to keep the spotlight off himself and put it on others, a lot of which was due to his insecurities.

"Trying to get it together man, believe me," Maurice suddenly said. "You just hit a couple slumps you know?"

Maurice's eyes darted around, avoiding eye contact at all costs. Derek felt as if he was sitting across from a distant relative rather than sitting across from his father. Image and reputation were the only things Maurice cared about most of his life; most times it was at the expense of spending time with his son. Gloria often asked Derek when he was younger if it bothered him, but he grew numb to it. The only factor that bothered him was that he felt robbed of having someone to give him guidance.

"I'm just tired of learning by trial and error," Derek once told Gloria when in high school.

After some time of watching television in silence and more small talk, Derek stood up and stretched to signify that he was preparing to leave.

"Headed out?" Maurice asked.

"Yeah, about to make a few runs. I just had to make sure I came by to see you."

Maurice nodded, not having much of a reaction.

"I appreciate it that man, really appreciate it," he said.

Maurice extended his hand to shake Derek's hand. After he shook his hand, he stood up to give Derek a hug, which was awkward and forced.

"I love you man, proud of you," Maurice then said as Derek made his way out.

"Love you too man," Derek said as he headed back down the stairs.

He did not feel much of anything from visiting Maurice, and never felt the need to share much about his life with him. *What kind of guidance can he even give me?* Derek thought to himself. *Trial and error continues…*

CHAPTER 18

Charlotte, NORTH CAROLINA

EVENING — 10:53pm

"KB are you listening?" a piercing voice disrupted Katie's daydream.

"Yeah girl, I am," Katie said lazily. "I am."

"You better be!"

Sabrina Vera sat on the floor in Katie's bedroom, her third glass of wine in her hand as she continued with her story. Sabrina was a part of Katie's inner circle, one of her closest friends whom she met during her first year at Darcy. She lived in West Palm Beach, Florida and worked for a software company as a programmer for a little over three years. She was only going to be in Charlotte for the night and of course, Katie agreed to let her stay with her for that night. She was always long winded when she told a story, and scatter brained so she often bounced around to several different topics. She also had a high pitched, soft voice, which sometimes made it difficult to hear her. Sabrina always spoke more aggressively than she was. Katie knew that if it ever came down to it, Sabrina was not built for serious conflict. They drank wine and talked in Katie's room for almost two hours. While Sabrina sat on the floor, Katie lay on her bed going over some notes from Sunday's message at church.

"I just don't understand, he just proposed to his girlfriend, and they just had another baby, yet worried about me and mad at how I move. Go take care of your family!" she continued with her story. "Is that not out of line? Monitoring and clocking me?"

Sabrina noticed that Katie was still lost in her own cloud of thought.

"Girl you are praying, let me leave you alone."

"No, no, sorry, I just needed to finish that; haven't read in a few days," Katie said, finally—but still reluctantly—closing her notebook. "I'm here girl."

"Nothing wrong with it, praise the Lord girl, amen. You can pray for me KB. I send prayers up, but they bounce back," Sabrina said, causing them both to laugh. "The Lord got me on 'do not disturb'!"

"Girl shut up, no He doesn't," Katie chuckled as got off of her bed. "You want some more?"

Sabrina stood up to follow Katie into the kitchen. The two of them comfortably lounged around the apartment, hair wrapped, no make-up on, and in their sleep clothes. Katie pulled out a new bottle of wine as Sabrina sat on one of the barstools at the kitchen island.

"You go to church every Sunday?" Sabrina asked.

"I try to," Katie handed Sabrina a full glass. "Definitely have to be there more now since I'm handling the greeters and hospitality."

Sabrina's eyes widened, causing Katie to shake her head and roll her eyes.

"You? Greeters? Don't you have to be polite to do that?"

"Shut up!" Katie smirked and took a sip of wine.

"I know God is real if you of all people are now greeting people at church, talk about a miracle?" Sabrina held her hand up as if praising the Lord.

"Okay, you're being dramatic now," Katie said as the two of them made their way back to her bedroom.

"You used to turn up with the quickness," Sabrina said. "And there was no calming you down, you used to scare me sometimes."

"Well, you can thank your buddy for that," Katie laid back on her bed, grabbing her phone.

After a few moments of silence, Katie glanced over to see Sabrina staring at her.

"Why do you do your dad like that?"

“Like what?” Katie frowned.

“Stop it, you know what I’m talking about. Your dad is an amazing person…and fine,” Sabrina shook her head as she reminisced.

“Girl if you don’t…” Katie waved Sabrina off.

“But for real, he is a good man. If it weren’t for him, we probably would not be friends right now.”

During their sophomore year of college, Sabrina went through a serious depression when she was unable to come up with the money for the spring semester. Her mother, who was a single parent, was in no position to assist her. The thought of not being able to see her friends again and leaving Darcy saddened her and her friends. When on the phone with Katie over Christmas break crying, Walter overheard their conversation and was moved to help. Walter paid for Sabrina’s spring semester as well as for her fall semester of junior year. All of Katie’s friends often put Walter on a pedestal and saw him only in a positive light. That memory of him was the last one her friends had engrained in their minds.

“Why are you so hard on him?” Sabrina sat on the edge of the bed.

“Hard on him?” Katie asked strongly.

“You *are* hard on him,” Sabrina said.

"Please, you just don't know. I didn't become 'crazy'," Katie used her hands to form air quotes. "As you say, until the end of high school. I used to be the apple of his eye; we had a real father daughter relationship. When I got older, started thinking for myself, and wanted to make my own decisions, he became the devil. He was so hard on me and critical of everything that I did, everything. Everything has to be done his way, and he's always right. He always tries to outdo my aunt and uncle lowkey. They are very successful; my cousins do big things too. People thought I was popular in school; my cousins make me look poo."

"But your dad is successful though. What does he need to be in competition for?"

"Not like my uncle and aunt. My aunt is a well-known successful author. I mean seriously established. My uncle is too, and my dad hates it though he will never admit it. I feel like he tried to live vicariously through me in a sense to compete with them."

"I get it," Sabrina said with a nod.

"Eventually I got fed up. I became careless," Katie said. "By the time I got to Darcy, I was turning up, getting drunk, high every now and then, all of that, and I was not for the games. I bit my tongue and suppressed a lot of how I felt so much back home, so nobody was going to disrespect me or walk over me. Anybody could get it."

"Trust me, I know. I remember some of those club nights."

"Don't even remind me," Katie grinned in pride and nostalgia. "It wasn't that bad though."

"Uh-huh, if you say so." Sabrina smirked.

"Me and my dad bumped heads because…and I hate to say it, we are almost one and the same. We are both stubborn and strong-minded."

As Sabrina's mouth formed to speak, she stopped when she and Katie suddenly heard the front close and two people talking.

"Hold on girl, hold on," someone said quietly.

Bianca peaked her head into the room, glancing back and forth between Sabrina and Katie. She had make-up on her face as if she had come from a night out, hair up in a bun, and two large hoop earrings in her ears.

"Okay y'all had a wine down without me!?" Bianca yelled dramatically, then nodded. "Ohh."

"Girl, grab a glass and come on," Sabrina said.

"Nah I'm just talking. I'm about to help my girl with these make up bag designs, later," she smiled as she walked back into the living room.

“She is so extra,” Katie rolled her eyes.

“Oh,” Bianca walked back in, eyes on Katie. “Girl where the cold drink at?”

“Probably out,” Katie shrugged. “We have to go to the store soon anyway.”

Bianca nodded and walked back out.

“Okay so, how are you and him now?” Sabrina asked.

It was evident to Katie that Sabrina was invested in the conversation; it was the least that Sabrina talked since Katie picked her up from the airport.

“Nothing has changed. This weekend will be the first time I’ve been home in like five years.”

“Are you serious?” Sabrina asked, eyes wide in disbelief.

“Dead serious. I was at peace with not having to interact with him or even have a relationship with him at all. I could handle him being critical and take his complaining. That wasn’t what got us to this point even though it was part of it. God really has been working on me with that though, that’s still my daddy so it’s not right you know?”

“I never knew all of this was going on.” Sabrina finished off her glass of wine.

“I don’t talk about it,” Katie said. “I was done with it.”

“It’s that bad to where you wouldn’t even go back home? There had to be something else. What else was there?” Sabrina asked. “What got you to this point to begin with?”

“Are you my therapist now?” Katie made Sabrina let out a loud laugh. “Like what is this?”

“This is just interesting to me!” Sabrina continued to laugh.

“To answer your question, apart from some other situations that happened, Isaac.”

“Isaac?!” Sabrina yelled.

“Isaac!?” Bianca yelled from the living room, imitating Sabrina.

All of them erupted into laughter.

“Please stay out there!” Katie yelled.

“Okay but you said by the time you got to college; you already were like this. So how is he a part of this?”

“I’m going to tell you. Isaac isn’t a terrible person, but at the same time, he is who he is. He is all about whatever can help him get ahead, an opportunist. If he was good, he didn’t care about what I was going through or things that he did to anger me. Our relationship was all about him and building himself up to get to where he wanted to be in life. He was with me for the doors that I could open for him—well, that my dad could open for him. My dad even bought him a gold Rolex, making it clear how good they were. I knew a lot of things weren't good for me mentally, but I dealt with it because I wanted to stay with him," Katie let out a frustrated sigh.

"Wow…" Sabrina's eyes widened again. "I never knew they got close like that."

"All the emotion that I put into that relationship was really for nothing. Yelling, cussing him out, fighting him, all of that was a waste of energy. It started making me lose faith in trying to fix any relationship. Me and my dad already were not in a good place, so that just drove an even further wedge between us. But that just accelerated the dark path I was already on when I got to Darcy. I'm about to tell you exactly what I mean…"

CHAPTER 19

Charlotte, NORTH CAROLINA

Two Years Prior

As the sunlight faded into the dim of evening, the incessant rain had finally run out, leaving behind a residue of trickling drops, and drenched streets dotted with shiny puddles. Katie lay on the couch, in the same spot she'd been in for several hours, listening to her mother Laura speak through the phone. Within those hours, she felt several different waves of emotion flow through her. She hadn't unpacked or moved anything else since Derek stormed out earlier. The argument replayed in her mind repeatedly, word for word, making her more upset each time she replayed it. Her eight text messages and four phone calls to Derek all were ignored. Katie hated being ignored. To her, it was blatant disrespect which she always took personally. Usually talks with Laura were all that Katie needed to calm down, but when Laura mentioned the name 'Isaac', it proved to be the opposite of what Katie needed.

“Why did you bring him up?” Katie asked.

“I thought you knew. He was just here,” Laura said.

“Excuse me?” Katie sat up quickly.

As Laura explained what happened, Katie looked at her hand to see that she began to shake. Laura explained to her that Isaac came by their home, and even stayed for a while.

“Why would you even let him in?” she asked angrily. “Why didn’t you call me?”

Katie began to pace back and forth around her living room.

“Your dad let him in. They were outside talking for a good minute, sounds like he knew he was coming. He gave me some lovely flowers, and he’s nice but… I wasn’t comfortable with it.”

Katie let out a strong sigh as she rubbed her eyes. She was speechless, nothing but profanity flooded her thoughts, so it was best that she kept quiet.

“I really thought you knew he was coming here, bold of him to just show up. “

“You should have called me when he pulled up, did he say what he wanted?” Katie walked to the kitchen and opened the fridge.

“He said he was just stopping by to say hello, but he was here to see your daddy. Most of the time, he was talking to him,” Laura told her.

“I just cannot believe this. I cannot believe my own father… you know what… whatever. I’m going to deal with Isaac,” Katie poured some grape juice in a glass.

“And how do you plan on doing that?” Laura asked.

“What do you mean?” Katie asked, annoyed. “I’m going to handle it. He is out of his mind.”

“Katie…” Laura paused. “Why do you get so angry?”

“I’m not angry!” Katie yelled. “I’m just…”

Katie put her face in her palm, trying to calm down. She began to feel an anger and frustration that she had not felt in a long time.

“Do you remember what happened your senior year of high school?” Laura asked.

Her voice was no longer that of a strict mother, but one of fearful concern.

“Ma, this is not—”

“No,” Laura raised her voice. “Tell me you remember.”

“I remember,” Katie sat down.

Laura brought up a time in Katie's life that she wanted to forget but could never. In high school, Katie and her high school sweetheart, Myles Gray, were a well-known couple not just at their school, but also in Houston. The two of them had been together since their sophomore year of high school. Although Katie was a sharp young girl, she was often naïve when it came to Myles, who was a nationally ranked football prospect. Having Katie on his arm was icing on the cake for him; she was one of the smartest and one of the most beautiful girls at their school, which had thousands of students.

Although Katie would hear rumors about Myles, she always considered it to be jealousy. While much of the jealousy came from her being with Myles, even more of it stemmed from Katie being as popular as she was and as well liked as she was. The jealousy heightened even more when during Myles' press conference to announce his commitment to play college football in Ohio, Katie sat right beside him along with his family. The conference was a few weeks prior to their senior prom. The evening of the prom began eerily when Myles told Katie that he didn't feel well and would not be able to go, which was odd to Katie but at the same time did not bother her. The idea of having down time to relax and be out of sight was much more appealing. Although she insisted on taking Myles some food and medicine, he continued to decline, telling her that it was not necessary. Katie, in her stubbornness, got in her car, picked up Myles' favorite foods, some medicine, as well as a few of their favorite movies. She also was anxious to leave the house because her and her father got into a major argument before he left town on business.

When Katie pulled up to Myles' house, the front door of the house was slightly open, enabling Katie to easily walk in. She walked past the stairs into the living room; she was very familiar with the house.

"Did you remember to bring the carrots?" Myles voice preceded him.

When he saw Katie, he froze as if he saw a ghost, eyes wide and mouth open.

"Carrots?" she asked, confused.

"What are you doing here Katie?" Miles asked strongly, putting his hands on his head.

"I brought some food and some medicine," she said softly. "If we're not going to prom, I can at least make sure you—"

The sudden loud cry of a baby interrupted her, causing Myles to rush back around the corner into another room. Katie slowly followed Myles, she could hear him pacify and try to quiet a crying baby. When she made her way around the corner into the other family room, Myles had a baby over his shoulder trying to rock him to sleep. Katie stared at the baby in awe, immediately touched at the sight of him.

"Whose baby is that?" she asked, eyes wide like a deer in headlights.

Myles was hesitant to answer, the sound of the front door closing caused Katie to turn around. Another girl walked in, a few years older than both Katie and Myles. Her face looked fresh as if she'd just washed it but also puffy as if just waking up. She had a plastic bag in one hand and her car keys in her other hand. Katie could clearly see a bag of carrots in the plastic bag when she glanced down at it. Katie also noticed how curvy she was, which Katie knew was always something that Myles had wandering eyes for.

"Myles, who is this?" she asked, completely looking past Katie as if she was not there.

"I'm his girlfriend," Katie said, stepping in front of her.

The girl looked at Katie and grinned, chuckling, revealing the gap between her two front teeth.

"His girlfriend? Aww…" she grinned then looked at Myles. "Why don't you introduce your girlfriend to your son. Maybe you need to explain to her what her place is."

Katie suddenly felt herself go numb as Myles laid the baby on the couch and stood in front of her. She could see his mouth moving but could not hear a word that he was saying as he explained himself. Myles met the girl, Laney, during a recruiting visit. One thing led to another that resulted in her getting pregnant. A few of his teammates, as well as some of the cheerleaders, all of whom Katie knew well, helped him to hide it from her. Katie had no idea how long Myles had been explaining himself, she felt as if she was in a trance.

"Baby I love you; I know this isn't right, I know it's not. What do I do though, what else could I do?" Myles asked, which was the first statement Katie heard him say.

Katie suddenly curled her hand into a fist and hit Myles in the face, knocking him back. She rushed toward him and struck him again, both of her punches drew blood. Before Katie could punch him again, Laney tackled her to the ground. As the two of them rolled around on the floor, Laney pulled a handful of Katie's hair as hard as she could, sending a sharp shooting pain through Katie's head. Katie kicked Laney off her and flung Laney around the living room once she got on her feet. When Laney tripped over the table, Katie pounced on her quickly, hitting her as many times as she could while calling her out of her name. Several of Laney's long fingernails broke from her fingers as she attempted to block Katie's forceful punches. Katie felt as if she woke up from a dream when two strong arms forcefully wrapped around her, pulling her off Laney. She realized she was in the large strong arms of Myles' father. The family room was in complete disarray. Katie's fists were covered in blood, Laney's face was covered in blood, and the baby was screaming crying at the top of his lungs.

"Myles, what is going on?" Myles' mother came in, distraught. "Katherine, what happened? Why are you…"

His mother stopped when she realized that there was a baby on her couch crying. She was at a loss for words. Two police officers walked in shortly after; the neighbors called them as soon as they heard the screams accompanied by things breaking in the family room.

"We received a call about a domestic disturbance—"

"Arrest her! She came in assaulting us, arrest her!" Laney screamed, causing them all to yell back and forth.

The officers had to yell over everyone to bring order and Katie was handcuffed. Myles' parents called Laura and Walter to explain what happened. When Laura arrived, tears immediately filled her eyes when she saw Katie in handcuffs, bloodstains on her clothes, her hair pulled, and a small cut on her face. It was one of the worst days of Katie's life, but the worst part about all of it was the scolding that she received from Walter when she talked to him on the phone. There was no concern for her well-being, he was not interested in what happened or the facts, he was so angry at Katie for how she conducted herself and he made it very clear. It took Katie quite some time to get over it, but she never forgot it. She never forgot how it felt, her own father to sound like nothing more than the next man as opposed to being one she could run to…

CHAPTER 20

"It was one of the worst days of my life, seeing you like that," Laura's words were difficult to hear, they cut deep. "I felt like I failed you as a mother, I just could not believe my baby did that."

"You never told— "

"Listen," Laura said. "I always feared that your anger would take you to a bad place. It terrified me…still does sometimes. When you left home for school, baby I had so much anxiety. It kept me up some nights."

Katie quickly calmed down. A heavy guilt washed over her hearing her mother, whom she admired and revered, say that she felt like a failure as a mother.

"Why didn't you ever tell me about how you felt?"

"I didn't want to," Laura said. "I tried not to let it consume my thoughts, it was anxiety I struggled with for some time. But now, I feel like you need to hear it. You cannot let anger control you. You are such a beautiful woman inside and out, but no one will see it if it's shrouded in anger. Stop letting people control your emotions and control you. You're upset and they are sleeping peacefully at night."

All Katie could do was take in what her mother said. She apologized and promised that she would do better and never make her mother feel that way again. As soon as she got off the phone with Laura, Isaac called her. When she didn't answer, he called two more times. Katie intended to answer the phone and unleash on him; it took so much in her not to answer. She declined the call and left her phone in the kitchen to avoid picking it back up, knowing that it would be trouble if she did answer. The conversation with her mother not only made her realize that she impacted others, but also that no matter how much energy she spent being upset, being upset rarely yielded a good outcome.

Charlotte, NORTH CAROLINA

Present Day | Katie's Room

Sabrina stared at Katie in disbelief; she could not believe all that she heard.

"That was the day I knew I had to switch it up. I'm not trying to make my mom feel like that again. It was also the day I made the decision to never speak to my dad again. What Myles did was a lot, especially for me as a girl in high school. That was my first heart break, and it was serious, yet my dad came down hard on me instead of consoling me or helping me process it. But then the fact that, years later, he chose to stay connected to Isaac, someone I walked away from for my own good, was another slap in my face. He just showed me where his loyalties were, and they weren't with his daughter. They still aren't, he is all about himself."

"Wow, that is just…man."

"Yep, so there's your answer!" Katie smiled and looked at her phone.

"Isaac found out where your parents stayed and went there, that's a little crazy," Sabrina said.

"He knew where they stayed, he's gone home with me before. Not many people know that, but he has been there," Katie said. "I didn't even tell Derek that my dad bought Isaac that Rolex. He thinks I bought it."

"So, what did Derek say about all of this when you told him?" Sabrina asked. "Is he nervous about meeting your dad knowing you two haven't been on good terms in years?"

Katie paused, and then looked up from her phone at Sabrina.

"I never told him."

CHAPTER 21

Dallas, TEXAS

Berry Residence

Tristan Berry sat in the middle of the floor, completely entertained by his set of toy planes and dinosaurs. He constructed an intricate scene in which the evil dinosaurs were trying to catch and eat the airplanes. Each movement was accompanied by a believably accurate sound effect. While Tristan was lost in his own imagination playing with his toys, Walter watched with a huge grin on his face. Tristan had a doctors' appointment that morning, so he was able to stay home.

"Walter, did you hear me?" the voice at the other end of the phone dragged him back into his corporate reality.

Walter was on the phone with one of his direct reports.

"Yes, my apologies, I'll be back in the office at the top of next week. I just need you to ensure everyone's numbers are lining up, many of the forecasts are incorrect and we need to correct them. Where are we with the adjustments?" Walter paced around the living room, dressed in sweats, a golf shirt, and his tennis shoes, which he rarely wore.

"Well, per Whitney, we're no longer going that route. He wants us to submit the forecasts as they are to meet the deadlines, and he says we will just make adjustments on the back end."

"No, we're not doing that," Walter said.

"We have to do it that way; they told us to adhere to all that Whitney has to implement. Matthias is backing him on this," the direct report told Walter.

"Submitting inaccurate forecasts is an ethical issue. How is Matthias even backing this?" Walter began to get flustered. "I'll deal with it later; I have to go now."

Walter hung up and tossed his phone on to the couch.

"Boom!" Tristan yelled as he crashed a toy plane into the floor.

Tristan then stopped playing and looked up at Walter due to the awkward silence. Walter looked down at him, and then began to grin again. Looking at his son gave him a moment of joy. Walter struggled to find things to occupy his time other than his job, it showed just how submerged into work he usually was.

Laura walked through the front door, accompanied by her parents as well as Jared and Olivia. Walter smiled as he walked over to greet his in-laws. Tristan, in excitement, got up from the floor to hug his grandparents. The kids were crazy about their grandparents, Glenda and Robert.

"Walter, looking good for an old man," Robert gave him a firm handshake and a hug.

Robert was in his late sixties. He aged very well, something that was common on Laura's side of the family. As Robert and Glenda entertained the kids, Laura gave Walter a huge hug. Walter was invited out for a few drinks at a bar that he and David, one of his fellow directors at Anomaly, would often frequent in their early days. When he informed Laura, she simply gave him a kiss before proceeding to talk to her parents. As Walter grabbed his keys on the way out, he could hear Glenda ask Laura when she could expect to see her beautiful grand-daughter Katie.

The bar was a decent drive, which was not too far from the Anomaly office. Walter played all his old school favorites as he cruised down the highway on his way to the bar. Katie taught him how to create playlists and find his favorite songs, and he stuck with it ever since she had shown him years prior. David was already at the bar when Walter showed up. The two of them sat at the bar for a few hours, having a few drinks. They were close colleagues and navigated through Anomaly together their entire careers, which caused them to grow close and learn each other's lives outside of work. David used to be overweight with declining health, but since became faithful in the gym and now was muscular and in shape thanks to Walter holding him accountable. The time at the bar was something that Walter needed; David was good for getting some laughs out of him. He always cracked jokes about work and other things. Even when David was being serious, he was one of the funniest people that Walter knew.

"You've got the lake house coming up right?" David asked before drinking his beer.

"Leaving tomorrow," Walter sat his beer down.

"Time is flying, that should be a nice little getaway. It's only Galveston, but it will still be a nice breather away from Dallas," David told him.

He and his family visited the lake house in Galveston when it was first purchased. Jeffrey and Janice both convinced Walter to chip in on it so that they could take their families there to vacation anytime they wanted. All three of them owned it.

"Yeah, should be nice. Katie will be coming, she hasn't been home in some years so I'm looking forward to seeing her," Walter said. "But she's bringing a friend so who knows how that will go."

"A friend huh?" David's eyebrows raised.

Walter glanced over at David.

"It's the kid she's dating right now."

"Aha, there we go," David signaled for the bartender to bring another beer. "I knew it was something. You don't seem too thrilled about it. First time meeting him?"

"We crossed paths at their graduation some years ago, but that's it."

"So… what's wrong with him?"

Walter took a moment to respond, trying to find the words to say.

"I love my daughter. We have not always seen eye to eye, we rarely ever do. But I will never stop wanting what is the best for her, ever. I have been where she is, I know what to do to be successful. I just feel like this kid does not have that for her. She just seems so lost in him that she is just floating through life with no ambition. Then I hear her rave and go on about him to Laura. I have never heard her like that. She has never even talked like that about me or shown that type of emotion at all towards family. So, I don't know, seems like she's into him… but I don't know what kind of security he can give her or if he's serious."

David stared at Walter with a straight face, not buying a word that Walter said.

"Wow, a real monster. Let's get our guns ready now," he said sarcastically.

"Shut up," Walter chuckled as he nudged David. "I'm serious; she has to be with a man that will make her better, not one that she is going to have to carry."

"But how are you going to determine that?" David asked. "I mean, I'm sure your daughter is much smarter than that, and is not going to put herself in that type of situation."

"You don't know her like I do. She's stubborn, very strong willed; it's hard to tell her anything, and she does not always make the smartest decisions. I can tell you that."

"I can't imagine where she gets that from," David made another sarcastic comment.

"Watch it now," Walter said strongly.

"Treading carefully here." David held his hands up to ease a bit of the tension. "But hear me out, you said you have never seen her show that type of emotion or love before. Maybe, just maybe, you are a little jealous?"

"Stop it," Walter snapped at him. "Just stop it, that doesn't make any sense. I have no reason to be jealous of a kid in his twenties who is in between jobs. This isn't about me at all."

"I'm not saying you are jealous of him; I'm saying—"

"Just stop it, you lost me with that one," Walter forced out a small laugh.

He tried to give off the impression that he was not bothered. David was no longer in a joking mood; he wanted to truly convey a message to Walter, whom he knew could be quite stubborn.

"Listen," David said to him, "My daughter and I had words when I first met her boyfriend at the time. I was not a huge fan of him at all, thought he was scum. I mean, he was trying to start a band, he did not see the point of working a job while trying to do so, I mean he was just… my goodness," David had a look of disgust as he pulled out his phone.

"What did you call it? Scum?" Walter asked, still looking up at the television above the bar.

"I'm white, shut up," David chuckled, making Walter laugh. "But, after actually taking some time and talking to him, stepping back a little, I realized that we were similar in a lot of ways, just a different generation."

David showed Walter a picture on his phone. Walter looked down to see a picture of David's son, his wife, and two small children, huge smiles on their faces as they were posing in a park.

"Now they're in Pittsburgh, married, kids, and she is so happy, I would not want her to be with anybody else. Their lives have come together perfectly. All I'm saying is, you need to give this guy a chance. Don't be so quick to hurl fire and brimstone on him, and you need to give Katie a chance too. She's your daughter, have some faith in her."

Walter stood up and pulled his wallet out of his back pocket.

"Thanks for the drinks," Walter tossed some money onto the bar and headed out.

David shook his head, signaling the bartender over so he could close out his tab.

"I hope you learn brother; I really do."

CHAPTER 22

Charlotte, NORTH CAROLINA

The couch in Derek's apartment was one of the most comfortable couches that a person could sit on; it was easy for someone to fall asleep within minutes of lying on it. Several of his friends had fallen asleep on it unintentionally during visits to his place. Katie sat, curled up on one part of the couch with her focus set on the TV. She was in sweatpants and a women's V-neck t-shirt. Her colorful polka-dot socks covered her feet, she was quite comfortable and relaxed. Before going to Derek's place, Katie spent a few hours at home ensuring that she was fully packed for their trip. During the week, the two of them rarely spent as much time together as they would have liked, so they made the most of each day.

Derek emerged from the kitchen, holding two bowls of ice cream. He extended one of the bowls to Katie, who frowned when she looked inside.

"Really?" she asked, looking up at him.

Derek continued to extend the bowl to her as he sat beside her and kissed on the cheek. Although Katie tried to act as if she didn't enjoy the cookie dough ice cream, the more she ate the more she looked like a kid in a candy store. Derek let out a loud sigh when he saw the reality TV show that Katie was locked in on.

"We really about to sit here and watch this?"

Katie's eyes were still glued to the TV. Her mouth slowly began to move to respond, but her attention was still on the screen as two women were screaming at one another. Derek then grabbed the remote and changed the channel, causing Katie to slowly turn to look at him with a smirk on her face.

"So, you chose rudeness today? Do I turn the game off when you're watching?"

"You watch them too though," Derek stood up.

"Yeah whatever," Katie playfully kicked Derek in the behind, causing him to thrust forward.

"You better work on that kindness if you're handling the hospitality at church," he said to her jokingly. "Be hospitable to me!"

"I'm about to throw this bowl at you if you keep talking!" she laughed.

"You all packed up?" he asked.

“I am, are you?” Katie asked, looking down at her phone.

“I’m all good.”

“Good, good,” Katie said, eyes still locked on her phone.

The change in her tone was obvious to Derek. The brief silence caused Katie to look up and see him staring at her.

“What, babe?”

“I’m just making sure you cool,” Derek said as he selected a movie for them to stream. “Real quiet tonight.”

“I mean… I’m just chill, slow motion.”

When the movie that Derek selected flashed across the screen, Katie let out a loud sigh similar to the one Derek let out earlier.

“Are you serious?”

“We never finished it,” he sat back down and wrapped his arm around her.

Katie seemed distant; Derek could tell that there was something on her mind. She was not her usual playful self, and just seemed to be uncomfortable.

“You sure you’re cool?”

"Oh my God, yes!" Katie suddenly lashed out, immediately wincing. "Sorry, I didn't mean to yell, I'm sorry," she leaned her head on Derek's chest. "I just had a long day."

Work was honestly the last thing on Katie's mind. She was mentally drained from playing out all the different scenarios of the upcoming trip. Throughout the week, she tried not to think too much about it, but it was inevitable. Thoughts of the trip gave her anxiety, kept her awake at night, and she had no idea how to deal with it. Derek also found himself playing out all the scenarios and possible outcomes of the weekend. However, the more he thought about it, the more confident he became about it. The competitive side of him began to view it more as a challenge to take on.

"I haven't been to Houston since AAU days," Derek broke the silence.

"We're not going to Houston," Katie said. "They live in Dallas; I haven't lived in Houston since high school."

"That's right, Dallas."

"But the lake house is in Galveston, so we won't be far from Houston. We actually can go up there for a minute now that I think about it."

Katie suddenly frowned as her nose began to twitch. Derek quickly realized what she was frowning about as the smell of marijuana hit their nostrils.

"Yeah, the people next door blow down heavy," he told her.

"I see; look at you, not even phased," she grinned, poking fun at him. "You go over there some nights, huh?"

"You know what, it's two chicks that live there. Maybe I should go say what up."

Derek quickly stood up.

"Ah-ah you better not," Katie stood up and wrapped her arms around him, playfully tackling him.

The two of them now stood face-to-face in the middle of Derek's living room.

"You're nervous about this weekend, don't lie," he said to her.

Katie looked down, silent.

"I get it's your first time bringing somebody home, but everything is going to be fine."

Katie looked up at him and his face made her smile.

"When did you become so optimistic?" she asked, surprised.

"I just prayed and let it go; God got it so why worry? God didn't give us the spirit of fear."

"Okay, I see you quoting the Word," Katie began to sound like her usual playful self. "Come on here!"

They both laughed. She began to feel better, which was something Derek was often easily able to do. The longer the two of them were together, the more confident she was in him and leaned on him for strength. She never leaned on anyone for strength in her life apart from her father. Once their relationship became rocky, she was forced to develop a resilience to be able to stand on her own, which did not prove to be enough. Katie fought a dreadful bout with depression while living in New York, despite having a fun job and being in an amazing city. It was an experience she didn't share with anyone. Between her breakup with Isaac and feeling a strong sense of isolation, the first year in New York was the toughest time of her life. One of her coworkers invited her to church one evening for a mid-week service. The message was about heavy burdens, coming to Christ for rest, and casting one's cares on the Lord. The message was one that Katie would never forget; it was the first time that she allowed herself to cry in front of others. After attending a few more services, she began to attend regularly and learned much about God as well as herself. She also began to attend therapy regularly while in New York to discuss her problems with someone.

"I need to go. Starting to get a little late," Katie sat and began to put her shoes on.

"Here we go," Derek said quietly to himself.

"Heard you," Katie held her index finger up, still looking down at her shoes.

"Come on, you might as well stay, we leave in the morning," Derek pleaded.

"I still need to make sure I have everything, so I need to go back home," she said, even though she knew she did not forget anything.

"You just said you are all packed," Derek continued. "One night is not going to do anything, nothing is going to happen."

When Derek said that; Katie stopped and looked up at him with a smirk on her face.

"It's not!" he tried holding back his smile.

"Umm… why did we have to set these boundaries again?" Katie asked. "How did we get to this point?"

When Katie said that; Derek conceded with the look of defeat on his face. A quick wave of memories rushed to his mind that he could not argue.

"Exactly," Katie stood up. "You already know."

"It makes more sense just to stay here and then head to the airport in the morning together," Derek continued to plead with her.

Katie grabbed his hand and led him to the front door with her.

"Just stop," she rubbed his cheek. "If we are doing this abstinence thing, it's better for us both if I go, trust me."

Derek's eyebrows raised and a grin came across his face.

"Oh, so you can't resist, huh? That's really what it is!"

"Boy bye!" She opened the door. "Be on time in the morning."

Derek sighed again, purposely holding onto Katie's hand as she tried to walk out. She pulled her hand away and walked down the hall towards the exit. Derek stepped outside of the door to watch her as she walked off.

"Say bruh," a voice behind Derek caused him to turn around.

A man was standing in front of the neighbor's apartment door. He wore a long black t-shirt that was clearly too big for him, jeans that were far below the waistline showing his colorful boxers, and a cigarette behind his ear.

"I got that gas bruh, fool with me," he said in a low voice.

Derek shook his head. "I'm good man."

"I got the pens too, just got those, selling em' for the low," the man continued, looking around as he talked to Derek.

The whole time he talked, he was digging in his pockets and glancing at his phone. His attention seemed split between several different things.

"You got it, I'm good," Derek said again before going back inside.

Derek chuckled to himself after he closed the door. He was surprised at himself; there was a time when he would not turn down the opportunity to smoke and would struggle to turn it down when he wanted to. He smiled because of the growth he saw in himself, but the last time he gave in was vivid in his mind…

CHAPTER 23

Charlotte, NORTH CAROLINA

Two years prior…

Tone's apartment was bathed in the aroma of candles and incense and shook with the bass from the speakers all around the living room. Tone and Trent, another of their classmates from Darcy, sat on the edge of the black leather couch playing the video game. They both yelled at each other and cussed each other out as they went at each other in the football game they were playing. Although Tone's apartment was clean, it was full of clutter from random unpacked boxes and jerseys hanging on the wall.

Derek stood in the kitchen talking to Elle, who was in the process of taking bottles of liquor out of a bag and sitting them on the counter. After leaving Katie's place and sitting at home for a few hours, Derek decided to go to Tone's house to get his mind off all that happened. Derek spoke to Troy about what happened while he was at home. Troy's response centered around forgiving Katie and hearing her out, none of which was what Derek wanted to hear. He knew his boys would see it his way and tell him what he wanted to hear at the time, which is what drove him to Tone's house.

"That's wild bro," Elle pulled a thick ink pen cartridge out of his pocket. "She probably never stopped talking to him."

Derek replayed it all in his mind several times, a mixture of anger and hurt would hit him each time. Preston suddenly burst into the kitchen, angrily looking at both Derek and Elle, sizing them up as if he was going to attack one of them.

"Man, if you don't get your little light bright bean head—" Elle immediately made Preston laugh as he shook his hand. "Fool came in here mad because he still can't grow a beard."

"Ha-ha-ha, that's funny," Preston said sarcastically. "Still knocking down more women than you ever have. What we in here talking about?"

Elle held his hand out, revealing marijuana in his hand that he dumped out of the pen cartridge.

"You good?" Preston asked Derek.

Preston also knew about all that happened, he was upset about it as if it happened to him.

"I'm cool bro," Derek said dryly.

“I been telling you about being the nice guy, didn’t I tell you?” Preston grabbed a cup. “You trying to be a good dude and she was out here moving fraudulent the whole time, getting it in.”

“She wasn’t smashing him,” Derek said.

Preston and Elle immediately looked at each other before looking at Derek. Elle shook his head as he pulled out a grinder.

“You a fool if you think he wasn’t knocking Katie off,” Preston persisted.

“Bro, she wasn’t on that,” Derek said.

“You don’t know what she was on,” Preston snapped back.

Derek quickly looked up at Preston but did not respond.

“But we not about to talk about her all night, we about to turn up and you turning up with us,” Preston said.

“I have to get up early man, I just came to chill— “

“No, nope,” Preston cut Derek off, putting his hand on his back to lead him into the living room.

Derek’s first Sunday on the keyboard at church was in the morning, it was also supposed to be Katie’s first time visiting GGC. However, his friends did not care to listen. After applying much pressure, Elle and Preston convinced him to stay and even to have a few drinks. Tone and Elliot invited some women over that they all went to college with, which made the night even more festive. They played spades, dominos, and other games, laughed, joked, and brought up old stories from school. Derek's phone continued to vibrate with calls and texts from Katie, which he continued to ignore. As he sat on the couch, the drinks began to get to him. Preston and two of the women debated at the table while they played cards.

"Y'all can say a dude gotta' be this tall, this skin color, look like this and that. You can say your preferences with no problems! If I say, I want a girl that got some yams and not a flat back and is a certain weight, 'oh Preston you a misogynist, you hate women'! All that bull—"

The women immediately cut him off yelling over him as they all continued to debate. Overall, Derek was having a good time, he felt like he was back in college for a night. A little after 10pm, the women packed up to leave after cooking and playing games for hours.

"We going to the club tonight," Tone told one of the women who asked about their plans for the night.

Derek had no intention of joining them. He saw the women leaving as the perfect opportunity for him to leave also and go home.

"Hold up," Elle stopped him. "You not leaving."

"I told you I gotta' get up early bro," Derek said, grabbed his sweatshirt.

"No, no, no, no, you are coming with us," Preston said to him.

"Turn up D!" Tone yelled from the kitchen.

"You haven't been out with us in a long time. It's not even a crazy out of control club for real, it's laid-back so you'll be straight," Preston assured him. "You will get back and be able to be at church in the morning."

Derek knew that it was not the best idea but had the strongest urge to go and hang out with them. After further convincing, he gave in and agreed to go. It was a much better option than sitting at home left to his thoughts, which was how Derek justified it in his mind. Derek was dressed in all black apart from his grey hooded sweatshirt; they told him that what he had on was good enough to get into the club. One thing that was noticeable about all of them was how well they dressed, whether it was casual or professional. Each of them kept themselves well-groomed, haircut, cologne, everything. Even when drinking or smoking, they never aimed to drink or smoke to the point of being sloppy or inactive.

Once they were dressed, Elle pulled out one of the blunts that he rolled earlier in the kitchen. When he lit it, Derek stood by the kitchen to distance himself from the smoke. They all insisted that he join them. All of them smoked together in college, Derek gave it up after his first year of college. He realized that he needed to give it up when he saw how much he relied on it. Derek showed up to class high several times. He even showed up to church high several times, which truly made him want to step away from it. He never felt comfortable being high or smelling like weed when he walked in.

"God made it, it's from the earth," Elle told him. "Weed ain' hurting nobody."

Derek eventually gave in; the familiarity came back to him shortly after and he quickly became mellow and relaxed. He smoked just enough for it to change his mood. They made their way downstairs afterwards, headed outside to the street where all their cars were parked. Despite having smoked and a few drinks in their system, none of them staggered or spoke with slurred speech. They had much practice in concealing it; no one would be able to tell.

"Trent, you didn't drink for real, you can drive," Preston said.

They all packed themselves into Trent's car. Derek's mind began to wander in millions of places, he had no idea what this night was going to have in store for him. As Trent drove close to ninety on the highway with the music blasting, Derek received two more calls from Katie, both of which he ignored. A few moments after ignoring the calls, he received a text message from her:

You are one of the most insecure and childish men I have ever met in my life. You keep ignoring my calls. Really? You are upset, yet you don't even want to talk about it or understand? I'm not babysitting or wasting time on a grown man who can't talk out situations. Maybe you should ask God to change that about you if you are a God-fearing man... right?

Derek immediately became upset when he read the message. He began to anxiously type a response, with every intention of taking as many jabs as he could.

"Whoa!" Trent sharply swerved as another car's horn blared in all their ears.

The swerve caused Derek's phone to fly out of his hand into the crevices between the passenger door and seat.

“You trying to kill us or what bro?” Elle asked Trent as he straightened up.

Derek reached down to grab his phone, letting out a sigh of frustration when he saw that the screen had a huge ugly crack down the middle of it. He never got around to sending the message that he started. Derek’s cracked phone screen added to the level of frustration that he had; he was fed up with the entire day.

When they made it to the club, there was a long line of people outside of the door. It was a one level square building, but the inside was a giant circle. The huge dance floor was a circle in the middle, booths and sections surrounded the circle, filling out the square shape of it. The bouncers at the front were tall and muscular dressed in all black, towering over everyone that walked in. There were already several people inside once they finally made it in, making it difficult to walk around. Derek was not a fan of nightclubs. He hadn’t been in years, but on this night, he just wanted to take his mind off everything. Preston and Elle knew a few people that had a reserved section, so all of them were able to post there.

“Get some shots!” Preston yelled over the loud music to Tone. “Just four; D don’t need none, he good!”

"What?" Derek frowned at them. "I'm good I can take one!"

"Nah bro, relax," Preston smirked.

Derek hated to look like the odd ball out, which was not something he had to deal with since he was usually not around. He just wanted people to see him as one of the guys. As Derek stood on one of the couches in the section for a while, he felt someone tugging on his leg randomly. He looked down to see a woman looking up at him smiling. She had a huge smile, hoop earrings, and she was in a tight black dress that revealed how curvy her body was. She waved at the others, greeting them as Derek stepped down and hugged her.

"What are you doing here?" she asked in shock. "I could not believe it was you, I had to come see for myself!"

Alicia Gary was someone they knew from Darcy; she was a year older and was always known for her body. She was known for being in shape and often posting provocative pictures on social media to show off her body, whether in the gym, out partying, or just outside. Derek often heard men talk about how they wanted to sleep with her.

"Why are you shocked?" he asked.

"Because… I mean, I just didn't expect you to be out in a club, and drinking. Are you drinking?" she pointed at the empty shot glasses. "There is no way."

"I show my face every now and then," Derek smiled at her as she rolled her eyes at him.

The two of them stood in the same spot making small talk for a few minutes, flirting, and playfully teasing each other.

"So, who are you talking to now?" she asked.

The moment she asked that question was the first moment that she did not have a full smile on her face. Derek was hesitant to answer.

"I'm talking to someone right now, we… you know," he said cryptically.

"You…what?" Alicia pressed further.

Derek immediately began to think about Katie, and felt the frustration and hurt come back to him again, emotions that he'd been able to block out most of the night. Despite all of that, he could not help but to pay attention to Alicia standing right in front of him. The DJ began to play slow songs and Alicia suddenly grabbed Derek's hand and led him towards a secluded area of the wall by the section. The sensual lyrics of the song led her to dance with Derek provocatively, moving her body against his. The two of them danced for most of the night and as much as

Derek did not want to admit it, he enjoyed it. Between the music, his friends, and the environment, Derek felt good in that moment. When he went back to the section, more and more shots were ordered, and he found himself drinking them to match the energy that was all around him. The conversation with Alicia was the last thing Derek remembered. Before he knew it, he woke up coughing and throwing up on himself. He lay in a passenger seat fully reclined back, looking up at the passenger window smeared with vomit. He had no idea where he was or who he was with.

"Where are…what time did we leave?" he managed to ask shakily.

A hand gently caressed his eyelids shut before he passed back out in the seat.

CHAPTER 24

Charlotte, NORTH CAROLINA

Present Day

The skies were heavy with clouds, and though sunlight tried to peak through, the frequent spasm of rain and persistent mountains of clouds would not allow it. Bianca and Katie picked Derek up from his apartment on the way to the airport. Bianca rarely interacted with Derek when they were around one another; the two of them kept interactions short and cordial. Like Katie, Bianca was a fast and risky driver, causing Derek to remain on edge as they drove to the airport. Bianca also played her music loudly, just as Katie did whenever she drove. Derek often grabbed his door handle to brace himself while Katie and Bianca were up front completely unbothered. Katie texted back and forth with Tasha the entire drive. She had serious anxiety the all the way to the airport and tried her best to keep it hidden. Derek, although a little nervous, was anxious to get the trip started. He had the same nervous excitement that he used to have before basketball games, a nervous excitement to face a challenge and show what he could do.

When they pulled up to the airport, Derek quickly got out to grab their luggage, relieved to get out of Bianca's car.

"I'm so mad that I can't go," Bianca said as she got out of the car.

Katie slowly got out of the car as Bianca walked over towards her. The two of them were far enough away from Derek to where he could not hear them. Katie's head was down as she rummaged through her purse, not making eye contact with Bianca. Bianca glanced down at the purse to see that there was not much inside of it. She took her sunglasses off and put her index finger under Katie's chin, lifting Katie's head up. Bianca felt a wave of compassion seeing that Katie's eyes were a little watery.

"I don't know why I'm acting like this," Katie let out a nervous laugh, wiping her eyes.

Bianca grabbed her in a tight hug.

"I love you so much," she said as she continued to hug Katie, then looked her in her eyes. "It will be alright; this weekend will be fine. Just remember, everything will happen how it's supposed to."

"Love you," Katie hugged her again. "You get on my nerves, but I love you."

Bianca was fully aware of the friction between Katie and her father but felt that what Katie was doing was right. Family was of high importance to them both. Katie felt better by the time she and Derek made it to the airport and through security. The challenge for her was staying out of her own thoughts. She usually had an iron fist when talking about Walter but being a few hours away from seeing him face to face shook her to the core, and she hated it. As she sat at the gate, Derek stood in line at a fast-food place to grab some breakfast for them. He was on the phone with Troy while standing in line.

"She is shaking, I've never seen her as nervous as she is right now," Derek said.

"I would have to see it to believe it, wow," Troy said. "You the first boyfriend she's ever taken home, right?"

"Yep, that's probably why she is so nervous. She needs to chill, I'm the one that has to impress. If she is this nervous, I don't have a chance," Derek said.

"I am really surprised," Troy said. "I'm excited to hear how this weekend plays out."

"Yeah, your entertainment at my expense huh?"

"Shut up, fool. You know me and the squad are rooting for you."

When Derek sat down next to Katie holding the two turkey breakfast sandwiches, a quick smile flashed across her face as she grabbed the brown bag from Derek's hand. What was most noticeable to Derek was how fragile Katie seemed. Her usual edge was not there, something that Derek was not used to. He struggled to understand why she was acting the way she was, especially since they were going to her family.

The cool air on the plane lulled Derek into a quick and peaceful sleep, mouth wide open. Katie was wide-awake, staring out of the window. She glanced over at Derek and grinned as a slight snore came from him before he readjusted and shifted his head. When Derek opened his eyes again, the pilot was beginning to instruct everyone over the intercom to prepare for landing. He glanced over to see Katie, who was staring down at her journal, adjusting the pair of thick black glasses that rested on her face. She was engrossed in a speech that she was editing for her friend Imani's art show.

"What? You pulled the glasses out?" Derek asked as he stretched and let out a yawn.

Katie rarely wore her glasses, against her doctor's wishes, but sometimes used them when reading, writing, or working on the computer. Although she had contacts, she was not a fan of wearing them.

“Yeah, we went through a lot of clouds, it was kind of dark and this light is still not the best.”

Katie closed her journal and put her feet back down on the floor. She battled back and forth in her mind during the whole flight but came to accept that what was going to happen would happen. Derek walked with a sense of confidence as they walked through the airport to get their luggage. As soon as they stepped outside of the airport, a huge smile came across Katie’s face. She quickly walked over and hugged an elderly man that came out of a black Cadillac. An elderly woman got out of the passenger seat with a huge grin on her face as well. They both looked much younger than they were.

“Hi!” the woman walked towards Derek, who smiled and extended his hand. “No, we hug; give me a hug.”

She gave Derek a tight hug. The woman had a very distinct and sweet aroma about her.

“I’m Katherine’s grandmother, Glenda. It’s nice to meet you!”

“I’m Derek. It’s nice to meet you!”

Derek then looked to see the man now walking towards him with his hand extended.

“I’m Robert, her good lookin’ grandaddy,” he laughed and gave Derek a firm handshake.

Glenda had the same hazel-colored eyes as Katie, which was the first thing that Derek noticed about her. Derek already felt much positive energy from her and Robert, who was a small slim laid-back man with a top hat covering his head full of grey hair. Seeing them was the first time all day that Derek saw Katie smile and be herself. As they rode in the backseat of the black Cadillac, Derek felt even more confident that all would be well.

"Derek where are you from?" Robert asked.

"Chicago," Derek said.

"Chi-town! Boy back in the day me and the fellas used to have a ball in Chicago, playing in some of the night clubs up there, maaaaaaaaan…" he smiled in excitement as he reminisced.

"You played in night clubs?" Derek asked.

"Yeah, I was in a band, me and four of my good buddies. I played the saxophone; we used to be all up and through Chicago, Detroit, Cleveland, good times!"

"Derek, please don't get him started; he won't stop." Glenda rested her head on her seat, staring at Robert.

"Well since I'm getting started, check this out. I did a show in New Orleans and guess who I snagged there?" Robert turned dramatically and looked at Glenda.

"Whatever!" Glenda yelled. "I enjoyed their music!"

"She enjoyed it alright, her life ain' been the same since!" Robert made everyone in the car laugh.

Derek began to discuss music with Robert and how he was able to play the piano as well as the drums. If Robert and Glenda were any indication of the kind of family that Derek was aiming to become a part of, he was all for it.

"How did you end up settling in Oklahoma?" Derek asked after Robert mentioned that they left New Orleans and went to Muskogee.

"Lifestyle changes," Robert said, all his enthusiasm went out the door at that moment.

Derek glanced over at Katie in confusion, who looked out of her window shaking her head. He hadn't been paying attention to where they were driving, but his eyes widened when he looked out of the window. The neighborhood they drove through was full of beautiful homes. They drove to the end of the block and pulled into the driveway of a large red bricked home, causing Derek's mouth slightly to drop.

"Ready?" Katie asked as she got out of the car.

The red-bricked house sat on a slight hill above the others around it, making it easy to spot the moment someone would turn into the neighborhood. A basketball rim with a glass backboard rested on two pillars above the three-car garage. A low brick wall ran alongside the driveway, caused by the hill. Derek also was amazed at how flawless the grass and the layout was. Nothing seemed to be out of place; it almost felt like it was not real. Despite Derek's amazement, he kept his composure, making sure he didn't look as if he wasn't used to being around nice things. Katie, standing at the open trunk of the car, grabbed her backpack and threw it over her shoulder. She suddenly stopped in her tracks, glancing at someone standing by the front door of the house. Derek could not stop staring at the woman in amazement; she was almost a spitting image of Katie. What also stood out to Derek was that she too had the same hazel-colored eyes. The woman quickly walked down and hugged Katie as if she was the prodigal son that finally returned home. While Derek enjoyed seeing the love spread, a nagging curiosity was in the back of his mind causing him to raise questions, but he continued to ignore it.

"Derek, welcome! It's good to see you. It's been a while!" She hugged Derek.

"You too, miss Laura." Derek glanced back and forth between her and Katie.

He still could not believe how much Katie looked like her mother. Derek was even more amazed at the house when they walked inside. As Katie and Laura continued to talk, Derek looked at the family pictures that decorated the walls. There were several family pictures but also many individual pictures in a certain part of the family room.

"Wow, ha!" Derek's reaction caused Katie to look over at him, eyebrow raised.

He pointed toward a picture of Katie at seven years old, wearing a football jersey, berets in her hair, and her front teeth missing.

"Yeah Derek, your girl thinks she's hot stuff now chile'," Laura caused Katie to frown at her. "Get on her about how she came from… humble beginnings."

Derek laughed.

"That's funny?" Katie glanced at him.

"It is actually," Derek said.

Katie's smile faded and her eyes widened as looked behind Derek.

"There he is," Laura smiled and began to walk in the direction which Katie stared.

Derek turned around to see a tall man standing at the end of the hallway, a little girl stood beside him with a cup in her hand. The man had a straight poker face, no emotion on his chiseled face. His presence was one that demanded the attention of whatever room he walked into. Derek's smile also faded when it got quiet in the room. The energy of the whole room immediately shifted. Katie took a deep breath, trying to relax.

"Yeah, there he is…"

To Be Continued…

AUTHOR BIO

Darrius Williams is a young aspiring author born and raised in Milwaukee, Wisconsin. Discovering his love and niche for creative writing at the age of six, Darrius has a true passion for storytelling and creativity. Apart from writing as well as reading, he enjoys everything sports, working out, and spending time with his loved ones.

Made in the USA
Coppell, TX
20 September 2022